Jeff Morris

The Dragon in Me

a novel of self-awakening

Vistastar
Halifax

Publisher's note: This book is a work of fiction. Names, characters, places and incidents either are the product of the author's imagination or are used fictitiously, and any resemblance to actual persons living or dead, events, or locales is entirely coincidental Reference to the Twelve Steps of Alcoholics Anonymous does not mean that Alcoholics Anonymous World Services, Inc. has reviewed or approved the contents of this book, nor that AA agrees with any subject matter herein.

Printed and bound in Canada by Hignell Book Printing
Editors: Suzy Waldman and Nancy Roberts
Design: Margaret Issenman ©2002
Dragon illustration: Kevin Sollows ©2002

Canadian Cataloguing in Publication Data

Morris, Jeffrey Hart, 1958–
The dragon in me

ISBN 0-9731657-0-7

I.Title.

PS8576.O7353D73 2002 C813'.6 C2002-904332-8
PR9199.4.M655D73 2002

Vistastar Publishing Company
PO Box 876, Dartmouth, Nova Scotia B2Y 3Z5
www.vistastar.com

The dragon sleeps in me. Its glaring eyes, supernatural breath and physical power are allies, capable of defeating my opponents and overcoming life's obstacles. Its fiery breath awakens my spirit. Learning to call on the dragon's power is my challenge. Sometimes the power flows with ease. Sometimes, it fails me, or I fail it. It is my mystery – the dragon in me!

This story is dedicated to my children –
Ben and Julie

Chapter 1

The late afternoon sun laid a golden blanket across the blackboard. This was Rob Ethan's first day of university and he didn't know a soul. He had reckoned the safest spot was in the middle of the small classroom.

A girl with long blond hair sat in the front row. She turned and glanced over the classroom, her gaze resting for a moment on Rob's black eye. Her hair fanned out as she turned back to the front and watched the professor enter the room.

"Aha! There it is. I thought I'd forgotten it," exclaimed a middle-aged man with longish grey hair as he dropped a stack of books onto the oak desk and snatched some papers that had begun to scatter. "And there it was all along. Good afternoon, ladies and gentlemen. Let's see who's here and who isn't," he said, putting on his reading glasses and scanning his attendance sheet.

But then he looked up confusedly at the students. "Did I tell you who I am?" He pulled off his glasses and smiled at the dozen-and-a-half students, now in focus. "Professor Arthur Sharpstein, Introduction to Philosophy."

After squinting again at the sheet, he popped his glasses back on. He called out the first five names on the list – all present. Then he squinted harder and exclaimed, "Mr. Robert Ethan, I nearly passed over you! Do you exist?"

In the middle of the room a hand drifted up; a dark-haired

young man seemed to be trying to use his other hand to shield his face.

"Quite a nice shiner, Mr. Ethan! I'm sure there's a story there. Where was I? Ah, yes – Mr. Julius Stein, do you exist?"

"Not before nine o'clock, but I do now," came a voice from next to Rob Ethan. A ripple of laughter followed.

"Please hold the applause until Mr. Stein says something profound," Sharpstein said sternly. "Mademoiselle Alana Stewart."

The blond girl in the front row raised her arm slightly. Sharpstein had to squint up and down the aisles before he caught her small gesture. "There you are. Nice to have you."

Alana tossed her hair over her shoulder and smiled brightly.

"Now I will explain what this course is about. Let me begin by raising some questions. Why does man exist? Does he exist? Does anything really exist? How about God – does he exist?" Sharpstein's grey locks dampened with sweat.

"What is moral conduct? Is happiness possible in this world? What answers did philosophers like Plato, Aristotle, Descartes and Kant postulate to these questions? More importantly, what are *your* answers here and now in 1975?" He hauled off his dull green sweater.

The hippie-looking Julius gazed over at Rob and scratched his head comically.

Rob thought to himself, I don't have the foggiest idea. But he didn't want to sound shallow.

"Does anyone know the book in which Plato wrote the myth of the cave?" Professor Sharpstein asked the room, propping a loafer onto a chair and putting his elbow on his knee.

One hand shot up; it was the girl in the front row. Rob straightened to get a better look at her.

"*The Republic*," blurted a soft voice with an English accent.

"Well done. Again, you are?"

"Alana Stewart."

"In his great dialogue *The Republic,* Plato claimed there are perfect things called Forms," explained Sharpstein. "Imagine a perfect circle that has no deformities. That's a perfect thing."

Julius winked at Rob, gesturing in Alana's direction. "She's a perfect thing," he whispered. Rob smiled reservedly.

"Forms don't only represent mathematical truths, but also moral ideas. They are the standards we strive to measure up to. Plato said the key to wisdom was to come in direct contact with these Forms. Can somebody think of another Form?"

"The perfect kiss?" Julius barked out, grinning as laughter erupted.

"You're Mr....?" The professor squinted at his sheet for the name.

"Stein, it's Stein," he hollered.

"Mr. Stein, you have been training more than your mind in pursuit of that Form." The class laughed once more.

"How about a perfect result on an exam, when you get all the answers right?" a girl with glasses in the second row asked.

"Let's think about that," Sharpstein responded with interest. "The instructor could have marked all your answers with a red check. But how do you know the professor has come into contact with the Form? Say he got it wrong. That might mean some of the questions he marked right were wrong, too."

"All there are, then, are subjective opinions about what is right and wrong," the girl protested. "The correct answer depends on who's asking the questions."

"That, my friends, is the problem Plato was trying to get around. We view the world subjectively, through our senses. But Plato proposed that the ultimate pursuit was to escape from subjectivity and sense the Form, whether it be a perfect circle, the essence of a rock or a moral standard we should try to achieve."

The girl shook her head in confusion.

"Let me try again," said Sharpstein. "Suppose everyone in this class were imprisoned together in a cave. Suppose I were to walk all day long in front of a fire in a cave next to yours and all you could see was my shadow on the wall of your cave. If I asked, what does Dr. Sharpstein look like, what would you say?"

As the professor glanced towards him Rob sank down in his chair. A student behind Rob raised his hand.

"You," Sharpstein pointed at the boy.

"I'd see a grey image on a wall."

"Interesting," Sharpstein said coyly. "Everybody who agrees with this fellow's proposition that you would know me only as a shadow, put up your hand."

Most of the class, including Rob, raised their hands. Not Julius; his eyes were half-closed and he seemed to be nodding off.

"Now, Ms. Stewart. Suppose you broke your chains and ran out of the cave and into the connecting cave where I was standing in front of the fire. What would *you* say about your knowledge of Dr. Sharpstein?"

"I would say that for the first time I had seen you as you really were."

"Handsome and well dressed, wouldn't you say?"

"Of course, sir. I would not say otherwise."

The class chuckled; Professor Sharpstein was pleased to have discovered his favourite student so quickly. "Excellent, Ms. Stewart. But if you had to go back to your own cave with a message for your friends, what would it be?"

Clearing her voice to get her confidence she said, "What everyone in class has been seeing is not the real Professor Sharpstein, and if they could escape their bonds they would see true reality."

"Nice! Plato would agree. Everything we ever see is a shadow of a Form. Once you have imagined the Form something reflects, you know it better. That is Plato's philosophy as to how we should live our lives – we should try to see the real world, which is a perfect world."

Rob sat frozen in his chair, his mind striving to understand the discussion. He felt stuck. Where was the practical guide that would explain how he might find a perfect world?

Rob left class with the other students and drifted towards the student lounge, a large, modern room crowded with buzzing students. Still trying to shield his face, he paced through the lounge, searching for an empty chair. Looking down at the carpet, he settled at one end of a brown vinyl sofa and began to read his philosophy textbook.

"Can I sit here too?" said a voice.

Rob looked up and recognized the thin, long-haired student who had been sleeping beside him in class. "That's cool."

"Julius."

"I'm Rob, how are ya?"

"Been better. I'd say we're in for some work." He collapsed his long body across his end of the sofa.

"Yup."

"Hey, what happened to your eye?" Julius asked, as he saw Rob from the side. "Did your old man beat on you? Mine does sometimes when he gets smashed."

This was too embarrassing a conversation. Rob shook his head and looked across the room.

Julius yawned. "I'm starting to think I should have gone to art school, man. Painting is a hell of a lot easier than staying awake through these lectures."

"You're an artist?" That was a safer subject of discussion.

"I try. What do you do for kicks?"

Rob thought for a moment about what might impress Julius. "Martial arts."

"That would explain your eye."

"Not exactly." Rob changed the subject. "What part of town do you live in?"

"South end, Cordova Street."

"Geez, I'm three blocks over."

"Neat. We just moved in – got the hell out of Toronto last month. My old man is a fuck-up. I thought – Winnipeg, I'm going to freeze my ass off and miss out on all the action back home."

This guy is really crude, Rob thought.

"I need a coffee. Get you one, what do you want in it?" Julius fished in his pocket for change.

Rob disliked coffee unless it had tons of cream and three or four sugars. But he answered, "One cream, two sugars. Thanks."

Rob wondered how Julius could stand to be so open about his lousy family. He admired Julius' boldness, but the possibility that Julius might strike up a friendship scared him – the guy looked like trouble.

When Julius returned, Rob steered the conversation away from personal matters. "You into disco?"

Julius hooted. "Man, disco sucks!"

Rob was ready to abandon this social effort, except he had to finish the coffee. When their philosophy class came up again, both agreed at length that the professor was pretty nice and the girl in the front row was a babe – though a snotty one, according to Julius.

Rob checked his watch. "Geez! I'm late. See you later, man." That last part about class was OK, thought Rob. Maybe they could be school buddies – but nothing more.

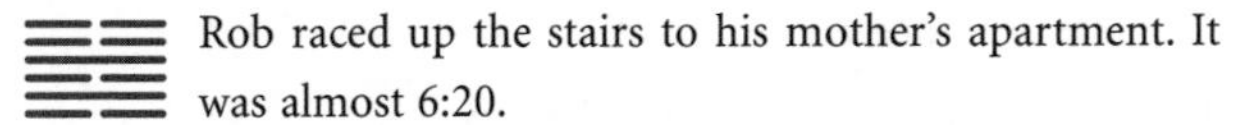

Chapter 2

Rob raced up the stairs to his mother's apartment. It was almost 6:20.

"Where the Jeezus H. Christ have you been?" his mother slurred. "You are supposed to be here at six on Monday nights. It's the only time we have together."

A bottle of Beefeater gin stood half empty on the kitchen counter next to the sink.

Catching his mother's glassy-eyed scowl, Rob was daunted by how her tipsy condition masked her dark, refined good looks. The long, black hair looked dirty, the makeup old.

"I was having coffee with someone from school. I am really sorry I wasn't watching the time. It was my first day at school."

"Why lie? You don't even drink coffee! Now you sound like your father. Always apologizing for being inconsiderate. I cooked you dinner. If you want it, it's in the garbage."

Rob dropped his backpack on the floor and took in the empty macaroni-and-cheese box and the dirty pot on the old stove. The sink was full of sticky dishes and the kitchen was cluttered with empty bottles, cartons and other trash. The linoleum was filthy with months of stains and grime. A large ashtray filled with cigarette butts decorated the middle of the kitchen table.

"Oh, your eye looks lovely, Rob. You're at it again, huh?"

"No."

"Yeah, right!"

Rob's mother walked to the sink and poured a large shot from the gin bottle into a tall glass, topping it up with soda. She shuffled back to the table and the glass hit the table so hard some of the drink slopped out. She mopped it with her hand. Flopping into a chair, she fumbled with a cigarette package, then with the lighter. The cigarette shook in her mouth while she tried to steady it with one hand and light it with the other.

Blowing smoke out, she said, "I ain't cooking anything else. You can cook your own goddamn dinner."

Rob stared at the clock above the sink and leaned back against the wall. He mumbled something under his breath.

"You got something to say? Huh?" Her hand arced through the air and cigarette ashes dropped to the table. "Forget it, Rob, you never have anything good to say to me. Don't waste your lousy breath."

This was familiar territory. Rob had learned not to suggest by gesture or word that anything was wrong with his mother's behaviour. It just made it worse. He already felt shameful for giving her reason to start up with him by being late. He promised himself again not to be so careless in the future.

"Would it be alright if I go?" Rob said softly, looking away, carefully keeping disgust from his face.

"I'll tell you when I'm finished with you for Jeezusss H. Chrissakes. You just stand there and let me finish."

His mother took two large gulps from her glass then pointed her finger at Rob.

"You don't give a damn about me. I just get evicted and you don't even offer to help me move outta here! I don't deserve to be treated like dirt. Your father treated me like dirt. You shouldn't be like him. Like he knows anything, huh."

Rob's mother butted her cigarette out on the edge of a dinner plate, missing the ashtray next to it. Brushing the ashes onto the table into a pile, she pinched them between her index finger and thumb and dropped the mess in the ashtray.

"I am sick and tired looking at your black-eyed face," she slurred, waving her hand in the air. "Go!"

Lighting another cigarette, she swore and muttered as Rob turned and left, closing the door softly behind him, thinking that living alone with his dad was so much better than before his parents' separation.

On the bus ride home, he blocked his mother's words. He repeated over in his head that what she had said was crap. Anger and upset were not supposed to be part of his existence any more.

Over the years, Rob had learned how to make his mind numb. But one diversion brought him fully to life. When it called to him, he indulged – and then afterwards hated himself.

Chapter 3

In the growing dusk, bright picture windows created a patchwork of rectangular lights down the street. Rob gazed into each home; when he saw people he tried to interpret what they were doing. A head watched television, people cleared supper dishes and two women stood talking.

The Ethan home was dark. The small bungalow had been white until Rob's father had painted it a putty colour shortly after his wife had packed and left. Rob had picked up a paintbrush to help, but he quickly became bored listening to his father talk about how badly he'd been treated by Rob's mother.

Rob stepped into the kitchen and turned on the light. He was still getting used to the new kitchen cabinets handcrafted from lightly stained oak. Mr. Ethan had not lost his carpentry skills, even though he was increasingly involved in the administrative side of his small construction business. Since Rob's mother had left, a constant hum could be heard most evenings from the woodworking shop in the basement.

Rob opened the cupboard. There was lots of new space for groceries but his father's shopping trips were spotty. TV dinners filled the freezer. It was long past the supper hour, but Rob did not feel like fixing dinner, so he took some crackers into his bedroom.

He emptied his backpack onto his bed and sat at his desk, trying to read an assignment for the next day. It was hard to concentrate with his mother's nasty mood playing on him. Sometimes he wanted tell her she was a lousy drunk leading a stinking life. But he could never bring himself to do that – it would only cause another fight, like one of his parents' screaming matches.

He tried to distract himself by thinking over his day. One pleasing thought was that blond girl in his class. What was he to make of Julius, though? That guy seemed screwed up.

Unable to focus on the book, Rob flopped onto his bed and shut his eyes. It was a chilly September night and he waited for the furnace to click on and warm his room. The cold evoked a memory of another chilly September evening.

Around his eleventh birthday he had been racing his new three-speed bike against his best friend Ben in the school parking lot. He knew he was probably late for dinner, but he had kept playing until it grew too dark.

When he had walked into the kitchen and asked his mother if dinner was ready, he had regretted his question instantly. Mrs. Ethan had consumed most of a bottle of rum, and her temper was on fire. "Get out of this house and find your own bloody dinner!" She had pushed him hard towards the door and he hadn't even had a chance to put his sneakers back on.

As Rob shivered by the back door, the sky had opened and cold rain pelted down. He had tiptoed down the sidewalk wondering where to go, with his socks soaking and his feet getting colder by the minute. He had thought of Ben's, but didn't know how to explain his shoelessness to Ben's parents. So he had sheltered on the back deck under a blue tarp that covered the barbecue.

After an hour he had crept back into the house and gone to bed.

Enough of that crap, Rob thought now. He jumped up, changed to his sweat pants and headed to the basement. There he stood in front of his *makiwara,* a six-foot-high board mounted to the floor by a metal bracket. His father had drilled holes in the bracket and inserted long bolts to strengthen the base. The bottom half of the *makiwara* went through the top of an old bald tire, and the top half was wrapped like a mummy with one-inch coarse rope. The tire on the bottom was for kicking and the top was for practising punches.

The Sensei had explained to Rob and a few other students that the aim of *makiwara* training was to strike the target and push it back as far as possible. The board would spring back, ready for the next blow. The students had listened intently to stories about the ancient masters who developed devastating power by training on the *makiwara* and became able to defeat armed samurai in street battles.

Rob started punching the board softly. He welcomed the pain – it was well deserved and a good distraction. As he hit harder and faster, the pain turned to numbness. Some red appeared on the rope, but he did not stop. Finally, he looked at his hands – his knuckles were raw and a cut on his right index finger had opened up.

A door slammed upstairs, and Rob grabbed a black towel from the floor next to the *makiwara* and dried up the blood.

"You down there, Rob?"

"Yeah, wait, I'm coming." He hurriedly finished wiping the blood from his hand.

"Working out?"

"Yeah," he called out on his way up the stairs.

Mr. Ethan was standing by the fridge, screwing the cap off a beer bottle. His black hair was greased back and he wore a faded jumpsuit over a dirty blue shirt. A carpenter's pencil was propped on his ear.

"How was your first day at school?"

"OK."

"Did you see your mom?"

Rob didn't want to get into it. "Yeah."

"How was that?"

"Fine."

"Was she drunk?"

"No."

"What happened to your hand?"

Rob looked at his right fist. A line of blood was running down his finger and dripping onto the floor. He examined the damage, putting his left hand behind his back so his father would not see it.

"Guess I went too hard with a punch. But it's OK."

Mr. Ethan took a swig of beer and wiped his mouth with the back of his sleeve.

"Some things don't make sense with you, Rob. Last Friday, you came home with a shiner. A few weeks ago you had a fat lip. Either this karate stuff is too rough or I'm not getting the straight goods. Which is it?"

"Sometimes I get sloppy and don't pay attention, and then I get hurt. That's all."

His father's look conveyed skepticism. Rob made himself a promise – no more detours after karate class. His appearance was raising too many questions.

Chapter 4

While Rob stood in line at the bookstore, he felt a tap on the shoulder. It was Julius.

"Hey, man. After I buy this magazine I'm heading home. Don't you live by me?"

"Yeah. I'll go with you."

The first few days of university, Rob had spent considerable time wandering around campus, checking it out. It was swarming with confident students in bright new T-shirts, and while he liked looking at those happy groups, he couldn't imagine he'd ever fit in.

Julius was weird, but he was definitely the friendliest person Rob had met so far.

They came first to Julius' house, a drab grey one-storey with peeling, dirty paint hanging under the eaves. The lawn was weeds and the flower beds at the front of the house were bare. A front window shutter was hanging crookedly by a single nail.

"Comin' in?" Julius asked.

Rob hesitated.

"Don't worry, my old man won't be here for a while." Julius chuckled. "Sometimes the bastard doesn't come home at all."

"I guess I'll come in for a bit, then."

Julius opened the outer door. Its screen was torn down the

middle, as though someone had deliberately ripped through it.

They passed the living room, where a woman lay in a purple housecoat on the couch, watching a soap opera.

"Who's with you?" she called out, not turning around.

"A friend."

"Did you clean your room?"

Julius didn't even answer. They clumped down the stairs to Julius' room, which was dimly lit in a red glow by a painted light bulb in the ceiling. Posters of Jimi Hendrix and the Rolling Stones were tacked all over the dark-panelled walls and tie-dyed sheets were tacked to most of the ceiling. The sweet smell of incense weighed down the air.

Rob only gradually realized in the low light that dozens of paintings were leaning against the wall three deep. Brushes and tubes of oil paint crowded a side table beside an easel. The paintings seemed to be all landscapes – mountains with black storm clouds threatening a deluge.

Julius shut his door, slid a small aluminium bolt into place and pushed open a small cobwebby window set high in the basement wall.

"Did you get Zeppelin's latest album yet?" he asked, passing the cover of *Physical Graffiti* to Rob.

"No, but I heard a song on it I liked. 'Kashmir.'"

As Julius put on the song and cranked up the volume, Rob flopped into a beanbag chair. Julius swayed to the mystical eastern beat. When the song was over, Julius slid the needle back to the first cut on the album and turned down the volume. Then he reached under his bed and pulled out a carved wooden box with a hinged lid, removing a small bag.

Rob squirmed, guessing what that was. His father was always giving him stern warnings about drugs; about how Rob would turn out just like his mother if he ever started. He looked over at the flimsy latch on the door. What if Julius' father or mother walked in? He wanted to leave, but couldn't think of an excuse.

Julius then took a shiny metal pipe out of the wooden box and pulled a pinch of dry leaves from the bag to fill the bowl of the pipe. He grabbed a lighter from his dresser and guided the flame over the pipe's bowl. Each time Julius inhaled, the marijuana made a second red glow in the room.

"Want to try some?" Julius thrust the pipe at Rob.

"Nope," said Rob quickly.

By the time Julius finished his eyes were glassy. He sat cross-legged on the floor, stacked some pillows up behind himself and lay back on them. Eyes closed, he slapped his thigh to the beat of the music.

As the track ended, Julius seemed to fall off his high.

"You know what? I don't feel like I'm going to cut it with university. The lectures suck big-time and the girls are too uptight. I don't even feel like getting out of bed most mornings. I don't even like painting any more."

Euphoria had given way to misery. A half-done portrait was propped up on the easel; a person with long hair and haunting, hollow eyes. Was it Julius?

"Who's the mug in the picture?" Rob prompted.

"I had no clue what to paint, so I started doing my own dumb face. It's crap, isn't it?"

Rob didn't know how to deal with Julius' attitude. It had definitely been a mistake to get involved with this guy.

"As for my old man, I wish he would leave. He's a bastard when he drinks. My old lady, I feel bad for. Her life is hell. At least I can paint, but she ain't got nothing."

"I dig you."

"Why, is your old man a drunk too?"

"No, he's not," Rob said pointedly.

Julius opened his eyes and looked at Rob. "Well, you got some kind of shit happening in your life, eh?"

Rob pushed himself up out of the beanbag chair. "I've gotta run, we got class early tomorrow."

"Sure. Oh, how about going down with me to the art gallery on the weekend? There's an exhibit by Jerome Johnson. Mostly prairie scenes, but groovy."

"Don't know. I may have to visit my mom."

"Doesn't she live with you? Your folks split?"

Rob hadn't meant to let this slip. "They might get back together. It's a trial separation."

"Sure, whatever you say. Let me know if you can come to the art gallery."

Chapter 5

On Sunday morning the bus was empty except for one lonely old lady in her church clothes at the front. Julius and Rob walked to the back.

Winnipeg's trees were starting to turn gold and orange, and small clusters of colour tumbled along the empty streets. The bus passed the legislative building with its stone dome towering to the sky. On the peak of the dome was the Golden Boy, a runner with a sheaf of wheat under his arm, gleaming in the bright sunshine. Rob envied the Boy's expression of joy and freedom. His own life felt like raw existence, by comparison.

From the bus they walked two blocks to the Enchantment Art Gallery. As Rob stepped inside, he smoothed his wind-ruffled hair.

They circled the front gallery to get an overview. After twenty minutes of Julius explaining various techniques of lighting and perspective, Rob lost interest. One painting seemed like the next to him. A photo exhibit entitled "Journey to the Roof of the World" in the next room caught his eye, and he told Julius he would be back in a few minutes.

Rob sauntered slowly around the large room of photographs. One that caught his eye was a portrait of an old Tibetan monk, his face chiselled with wrinkles. The holy man was wearing a wine-red robe and sitting at peace in lotus position. Impressed by the photo, Rob decided to start at one end of the exhibit and take in each photo fully.

He began with an image of Mount Everest towering over the clouds, snow reflecting sunlight while the lower elevations got only shafts of sun. Before long, however, he became distracted by two other people in the gallery. They were an older man and a girl about his own age at different places in the room. The girl had blond hair held back by blue clips and she was wearing a blue oriental dress made out of silky material.

The girl was slowly touring the exhibit from the opposite end, so they gradually came closer to meeting up in the middle. When they were feet apart, Rob met her eyes for the first time. As he had suspected, it was Alana. Her eyes were the same strong blue as her dress.

Finally they were standing side by side, both studying yaks grazing against a background of snowy peaks.

"Stupid-looking beasts, aren't they?" she criticized.

"Yeah, but the mountains are awesome," he said, trying to sound intelligent.

"They're even more inspiring when you see them for real," she smiled.

"I can dream. Why, have you been there?"

"We travelled through Tibet on our way to Japan last summer."

"Wow! I would love to climb Everest."

"We only made it as far as base camp, but that was enough for me. It takes time to get accustomed to such high altitudes. Incidentally, my name is Alana." She held out her hand.

"I know," he blurted – and instantly realized she didn't remember him at all.

"How? Are we acquainted?"

"I'm in your philosophy class. I sit at the back beside the guy with long blond hair."

"I certainly remember him!" She chuckled. "And you're the bloke with the black eye."

Rob cringed and changed the subject. "You have a pretty strong accent. Did you just move here?"

"Yes, from England. My father started a job at the university this fall, teaching Asian studies."

"What other classes are you in?"

"I'm studying sociology. And also Eastern religions – my father brought me here to see this exhibit."

Rob realized he shouldn't take this girl away from her father for too long. "Well, enjoy the rest of it."

"I sure will. You too. See you in class." She gave him a parting smile and moved towards her father.

Rob stared at her from behind. He felt light and heavy at the same time. Surely it was not possible to fall in love with someone so quickly. But could her friendliness mean that she might be attracted to him, too?

Rob assessed whether he would have sounded interesting or boring at each point in their conversation. He concluded that he had been mostly boring and was probably not good enough to be with her.

He went back into the other gallery to find Julius.

"Where have you been, man? I finished ages ago!" Julius whispered loudly.

"You'll never guess who I saw here."

"I don't know, Olivia Newton-John?" grinned Julius.

"Close," Rob smiled. "Alana."

"Who?"

"The blond girl from philosophy class."

"Piss off."

"I'm not kidding. We had a nice chat."

“She’s a babe! Think you can score?”
Rob’s self-doubt returned. “Geez, I don’t know.”
“Sit next to her, I dare you.”
“We’ll see.”

Chapter 6

Rob had worked out a plan – if Alana smiled he would sit next to her, otherwise he would proceed to the back with Julius.

Julius approached the bus stop in a soiled jean jacket and a ball cap. The guy was sloppy, Rob thought, but there was no point in being judgmental. A friend is a friend.

"You still all hot and bothered about Alana?"

"Possibly. What's it to you?"

"I've decided that I'm going for her."

"What!" So this was his supposed new friend. A complete jerk!

"I'm more her type," Julius said.

"How the hell do you know?"

Julius' poker face broke into a wide grin. "Take it easy, man, I was just kidding."

Rob folded his arms and looked off.

"Dude, can't you take a joke?"

Rob forced a smile. "Jerk!" He punched Julius in the upper arm, harder than he had intended to.

"Man, that hurt! What are you, a black belt or something?"

Sharpstein was wiping off the blackboard when they arrived in class. Rob looked around but Alana was not in her usual location. Instead, there was a big girl in a football sweatshirt in the front row. Damn!

As Rob started to walk to the back, Julius made a little sideways gesture. There was Alana, at the other end of the front row. She gave him a slight smile of recognition. Now he was in for it – he had to walk all the way across the front of the room to sit beside her.

He tried to look casual as he slid into the desk. Alana's hair was pulled back into a ponytail and Rob caught the light scent of perfume.

"Where is everyone?" Sharpstein said, pounding the desk for attention. He looked at the clock. "Let's get into it. Those who aren't here will have to miss out on our collective wisdom."

He wrote the word "God" in big letters on the blackboard, along with a question mark. "So, who in the room believes that God exists?"

Half the class put up their hands.

"And who doesn't believe that God exists?" A third of the students put up their hands.

"Now, how many don't know?"

Rob's raised his arm slightly. Alana glanced over; she had been one of the believers.

Sharpstein scribbled the results of his poll on the blackboard. "A nice diversity here, all sorts of people. Miss Simpson, would you please describe Thomas Aquinas' proof of God's existence."

The smart girl with the big glasses glanced at her notebook. "The world is so complex that each part can only operate properly if all the other parts operate properly. Thus, there has to be a creator, because it is all too perfect to have happened by chance."

"Excellent. Now! Who wants to argue with Miss Simpson?"

"You," said Sharpstein, pointing at a freckled student in the third row.

"Can't we explain that complexity through evolution, as genetic changes occur that help the different parts adapt to their environment and are passed on to the next generation?"

"Explain."

"The parts can start behaving more successfully over time without knowing why, so after a long time the whole seems almost perfect."

"Who wishes to argue against this young man, on behalf of God?" Arms flew up. "Back row, red shirt."

"It's simple. God created the universe, so he must exist," a guy with a brush cut said pompously. A few students groaned.

"Defend your proposition!" Sharpstein ordered.

The guy read from his notes. "Everything must have a cause, so somewhere there has to be a first cause of everything. God caused everything else but isn't caused by anything, so he must be the first cause."

"Yeah? What about the big bang?" shouted Julius from the back.

The guy with the red shirt was bursting to defend himself, so Sharpstein gave him a nod.

"You still had to have God to set off the big bang."

"Sure, man, and how the hell could God create himself?" contributed Julius.

"He's always existed!"

"Oh, yeah, and did he create the devil too?"

"Burn in hell then, fool," said the boy, twitching with anger.

Julius sat back with a smirk.

Sharpstein raised his hand. "Let's move on, shall we? Your reading assignment discussed the ontological argument for God's existence. Who can repeat it? You, black shirt in the front row."

Rob looked down at his notebook but couldn't find the answer. Why did he have to be picked this time! "Sorry, I don't remember."

"The young lady sitting next to him … ah, Ms. Stewart?"

Alana spoke out in a clear voice. "We all can think of a perfect being. The being would be even more perfect if it truly existed. Therefore God, who is the perfect being, must exist."

"Responses?"

Rob's arm shot up. Something had come back to him from the reading.

"The man in the black shirt, whose mind was previously blank," said Sharpstein, drawing a chuckle from the class.

"Why does God permit such terrible suffering in the world if he's perfect? I mean, people beat other people up and everywhere there's booze, drugs and crime. If there is a God, he sure isn't perfect. So that argument doesn't work."

"Mr. Red Shirt at the back. What can you say to this atheist?" quipped Professor Sharpstein.

"You can't blame God if man screws up, because God gave man free will!" he said indignantly.

"Yeah, but when children starve to death, how is that free will?" Rob challenged.

Red Shirt stuck to it. "That God didn't make a world we see as perfect doesn't mean he isn't perfect. Natural disasters sometimes bring out good in people, with neighbours helping each other and caring for those who get hurt. Besides, those who die enter the Kingdom of Heaven where they get to be full of bliss."

"That's crap," Julius blurted, with Rob silently agreeing. He wasn't buying the Kingdom of Heaven idea. Once you're dead, that's it.

"End of class, folks. Read chapter three for next time," Sharpstein said, brushing off the chalkboard.

"See you at the next class, Mr. Atheist," Alana teased, smiling, on her way out, but Rob was lost in thought. Then she was gone, and he had missed the opportunity to defend himself against her reproach.

"Damn," he muttered, running his fingers through his hair.

Chapter 7

 "Rob, we're going now. Don't forget the present on the kitchen table."

"Do I have to go?" It was Saturday, and Rob usually didn't have to visit his mother on the weekend.

The answer was another volley of knocks on his door.

Rob had difficulty prying his body from bed. He had been revisiting each encounter he'd had with Alana that week. Her friendliness was so confusing, he thought, and forced his face deep into the soft feathers. Then, short of breath, he rolled over on his back.

Rob stared out the car window as his father silently drove towards the North End. They never talked about his mother's drinking. It was always just there, hanging over the family.

Before the separation Rob's mother had been able to deal with daily life. But now she was drinking worse and sliding into a paralyzing misery. She had just moved into a single-room apartment in a falling-down house. As they drove closer, Rob noticed the desperate people on the street and his spirits sank.

Two second-floor windows on his mother's building were boarded over. An old stained mattress leaned against the porch and fast food wrappers were strewn on the front grass. A scraggy orange cat guarded the entrance from a window ledge.

Rob's father looked like he wanted to apologize for leaving him there. "I'll pick you up in an hour."

"Don't be late, alright?"

Rob's stomach turned from the sickening odour of cat piss inside the front door. Rotting garbage filled a metal can in the vestibule and the stains on the wall near the mailboxes looked like blood.

At room six he knocked lightly. Noise stirred behind the door, then it opened. His mom's long dark hair and striped dress were unkempt, but to Rob's relief she wasn't drunk.

She took the present from his hands, hardly looking at it. Then Rob heard a man's voice in the room and stepped back into the hallway.

"Rob, don't be shy," she said, tugging Rob's arm. A middle-aged man with long, greasy black hair was sitting on the bed fumbling with the last few shirt buttons. "Rob, this is my friend Sonny." A crooked nose and a wide scar above his left eyebrow accented the man's pockmarked face.

Sonny got up and gripped Rob's hand tightly with cigarette-stained fingers. "Nice to meet you, Rob. See ya later, doll," he said, revealing a missing front tooth. A coughing spell receded down the corridor with him.

Rob was sickened at his mother's choice of company. Her faded good looks contrasted with her friend's homeliness. Rob also did not care for her low-cut dress; it made her look cheap.

"Happy birthday."

"I don't know what's happy about it, kiddo. I think I'll just stay thirty-nine for a while." She set the blue-and-gold-wrapped box on the kitchen table and lit herself a cigarette.

Rob couldn't believe that after he'd made himself come, his mother wasn't even interested in the present. "Were you going to open my present?"

"Yes, it's probably the only one I'm getting." She ripped the paper and lifted the lid of the box, then put it back down on the table. Apparently she didn't like the pink slippers. "So … you doing good in school?"

"Fine."

She looked more cheerful. "Want me to heat up some chocolate milk for you, the way I used to?"

Rob was surprised his mother had bought him chocolate milk. Her hand shook while she opened the new carton and poured the milk into a saucepan.

Rob's mother sat in the only kitchen chair and smoked as the milk warmed. After a minute she poured it into a Styrofoam cup. Rob was grateful that he didn't have to stomach it in one of the dirty mugs and glasses strewn around the sink area. He moved to the torn sofa and sipped his drink.

"How's your father?"

"OK. He's going hunting in the morning."

"What else is new? Has he got a girlfriend?"

"No."

"He should, he's not a bad guy." She looked out the window. "Does he still nag you about everything?"

"Sometimes, I guess."

"You know, my new friend Sonny used to box, years ago. You could show him some of that chop-chop stuff."

"OK, far out." He was surprised she even remembered.

"Get your black belt yet?"

"Nope, soon maybe."

"What's taking you so long?"

Rob shrugged. He hated when his mother criticized him.

"Talk to your aunt?"

"Nope."

"She never calls me either."

Rob guessed that his aunt and uncle were avoiding his mother. Aunt Patty was a kind lady and devoted to her family, but Uncle Phil was more judgmental.

He needed a break. "Mom, where's the bathroom?"

"Down the hall on the left."

Rob crept down the smoky yellow hall and found the bathroom. The smell of vomit in the sink turned his stomach.

The memory of the night his father left on a hunting trip flooded in while he stared into the mirror.

Rob had awakened feeling sick. He hadn't had time to make it to the bathroom and had thrown up on his bed. He wasn't sure whether to wake up his mother or not. Finally, he had tiptoed to her room.

Light had shone under the door. Oh, good, he had thought, she's awake. But when he had pushed the door open his mother had jumped up, screaming at him to get out. Rob had glimpsed a strange man in the bed.

Rob had hurried to his bedroom, scared to death. He had rolled up the smelly bedding and put it in the closet. The rest of the night he had kept waking up, shivering and sick, but was afraid to go the bathroom in case he saw that man again. He used the wastepaper can by his desk.

In the morning, he had trembled when his mother cursed at him for the mess in his room. She had asked if he remembered going into her room during the night, and Rob had said no.

Stepping back into his mother's apartment, Rob saw she was wearing the new slippers as she washed a mug.

"What took you so long, anything wrong?"

"No."

"Let me see you." She turned from the sink and took a good

look at him for the first time. "You look skinny. Are you eating enough?"

"Yes, Mom, I'm fine. I eat a lot."

"Your father doesn't know how to cook. I'll bet if you were staying with me you'd eat a lot better. Maybe if I got a nicer place you could live with me?"

"You are a lot further away from the university."

"Say I got a two-bedroom near the university and you could walk to class. That would be even better, hey?"

He knew she was testing his feelings about her. He doubted she was in a financial position to move to the university neighbourhood. He had to exercise caution telling his mother he would not be willing to relocate to her home.

"I'm not sure, Mom. I think Dad kind of likes having me around."

Mrs. Ethan glared at him coldly and went back to her tidying-up. In silence she dumped the rest of the hot chocolate. Rob looked at his watch; fifteen minutes to go.

"Well, I gotta go, Mom, Dad's coming now." She didn't turn around.

"Thanks for the hot chocolate. 'Bye."

Rob walked around the block to kill time. His mood sank. What a loser he was.`

There was only one place Rob felt alive, but each time he went there he hated himself more.

Chapter 8

The Saturday karate session ended at 5:00. Rob walked down the stairs from the dojo, his heart pounding with a familiar excitement.

At the bottom of the stairs he told himself he'd better turn right. But he stood in the cold wind and light shower looking indecisively towards his bus stop.

He walked left. Now his excitement grew with each step; there was no turning back. He jogged down to the intersection with Main Street, the streetscape growing brighter and louder. Where the Occidental Hotel sign blinked in red neon, he walked into a smoky lounge.

He was hit by the stench of beer but then the darkness seemed to mask it. He sat on a round bar stool and finished up one whiskey and coke, then another. But he knew he could stop – he wasn't a drunk like his mother. It wasn't the booze he craved.

Back on the street he was in the minority. Rob knew about the Cree, the Ojibway and the Dene. They had been the warriors of the prairies, but they had been poisoned by the bigotry and booze of the white man. So Rob would let the street carry out its justice.

Rob scanned the street; three young men were heading his way. He stepped back against a corner store until they passed and turned the corner. A minute later two of the guys came back his way.

Two, he thought, just right. When they were within feet of him,

Rob stepped out and collided with the larger guy.

The big guy angrily tried to push Rob away, but Rob dropped down in his stance and drove both of the guy's arms in the air.

"Motherfucker. What're you on, eh?"

"I'm only seeing how tough you really are."

The guy threw a punch, which Rob blocked. His buddy sent an undercut into Rob's ribs and Rob kicked him in the balls. The big one swung wildly. He missed once but then connected with Rob's right ear. It stung like hell and Rob lost his footing, slamming against the brick wall of the convenience store. Five or six blows rained down on Rob's body; he had taken enough.

"OK, I'm done," Rob gasped, dizzy.

"We ain't done with you, chickenshit."

Realizing he was in trouble, Rob readied himself. The two guys charged at him swinging and kicking. Rob connected a back fist to the tall guy's nose and then kicked the smaller one's knee.

His counterattack opened a window of escape. The two guys pursued Rob back towards the intersection, but he made it off their turf and kept running toward the bright red sign of Sal's Diner.

The familiar display case of Jell-O and pies was a welcome sight. Sitting in a booth at the back, Rob ordered a burger. His ear throbbed and his hearing was dull so he fished some ice cubes out his water and cupped them to his ear.

That had been close; he vowed not to go down Main Street again.

Chapter 9

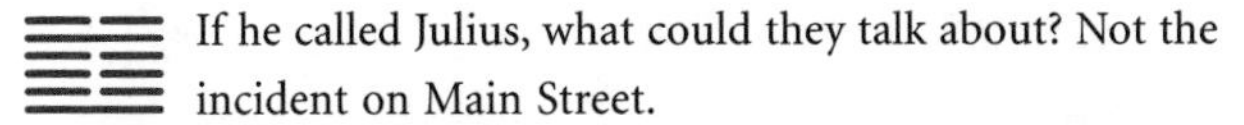

If he called Julius, what could they talk about? Not the incident on Main Street.

Rob stared at the phone. It was Saturday night, and he had nothing to do.

For two weeks he and Julius had been walking or riding the bus together and chatting in the lounge between classes. School was safe territory, but he still wasn't sure about friendship. Julius could be up or down and funny or sad – Rob never knew which until he saw him.

Rob drew a few spirals around the phone number and lifted the receiver. He tensed as Mr. Stein answered.

"Is Julius home?"

"Hold on … Julius! Answer the goddamn phone! Where the Christ are you?"

Rob twisted the phone cord in knots while nothing happened on the other end.

"Are you going to answer the bloody phone? Christ almighty, where the hell is that kid?" The receiver dropped with a thud and Rob heard muffled cursing.

"Hello?" Julius said, just as the first phone slammed down.

"It's Rob."

"Jeezus, Rob, how are you, man?"

"Fine, sorry to bug ya, I was just wondering if maybe we could do something, if you weren't busy or anything."

"You can't come over here cuz my old man's half pissed. Come get me and we'll go to Angelo's."

In a few minutes Rob was standing in front of Julius' house hoping not to run into Mr. Stein. There was a green Chevy in the driveway with two hubcaps missing and a crunched rear bumper. Rob thought, what a rustbucket.

Julius burst out the door, his hair flying out horizontally in the wind. "Let's get out of here."

"Why?"

"Start walking! I was taking some allowance out of my old man's wallet and he walked in as I was shutting the drawer. He's counting his money right now."

What would Julius be in for when he got home, Rob wondered.

Angelo's was an Italian family restaurant with red-and-white-checkered tablecloths, wine bottles lining the walls and the phone ringing in takeout orders. Rob and Julius sat in the front window. A dark-haired girl came over and lit their candle, which was stuck in a bottle covered with wax drippings.

"Be right back, boys," she said, slapping the menus down.

"Pepperoni, sausage, onions and green peppers, how about it?" Julius said, putting down his menu.

"Cool, my favourites too. Extra cheese?"

"Right on. She's a babe," Julius said, nodding at the waitress.

Rob chuckled and made a remark about her sexy shape.

The dark-haired girl came and took the order, and Julius gawked at her rear as she walked towards the kitchen. "Nice. So when are you going to score with Alana?"

"I'm just warming up, man. I haven't got to first base yet."

"You gotta get your bat out first, if you can find it," Julius ribbed.

"Once I get it out, I know how to use it."

"I bet you've never had a hit."

Rob looked down at a cigarette hole in the tablecloth. "So … why didn't you want me to come over to your place, man?"

"Usual bullshit. Saturday night's my old man's big piss-up night, cuz my mother doesn't bitch about it. I know if I look at him the wrong way, I better be ready to run.

"Yeah, I dig."

"You put up with that shit from your dad?" Julius said, gripping the white cloth napkin.

Rob felt the urge to leave the topic alone, but he kept talking anyway.

"Let's say my mother is a major aggravation sometimes."

Julius balled up the napkin and tossed it into the air. "Not in my house. My dad's a bastard. He used to beat on me, but now he picks on my mother most of the time."

"My parents used to scream at each other after my mom got drunk, that was about it. Though my mom did throw the occasional plate at my dad."

"At least your parents split up; mine are still together. So I gotta get out of there somehow."

"How come you don't?"

"When we were in Toronto I was supposed to go to art school, but my old man said he couldn't afford it after the bank took the house. Now he's working in my uncle's carpet business and there's no chance in hell. So we're all stuck in that crappy little house together."

After they had finished off the pizza they wandered towards their streets. Julius picked up a fallen tree branch and hit every lamp-post with the stick. Reaching Julius' house, they slapped hands.

"You going to be OK?" Rob asked.

"Yeah, the car's gone; he won't be home till tomorrow. Christ, he'll never remember what happened."

Rob walked on, slowing his pace only when he got to his own block. He gazed down at the ice filling the cracks between the sidewalk slabs; it seemed to be shimmering in the dark.

His parents had had some hot arguments, but he could not remember his father ever touching his mother. Maybe his life was not necessarily any worse than anyone else's?

Still, he remembered one night when he was nine and his mother had come home late from a bar. The screaming was fierce; dishes and bottles smashed in the kitchen; the back door slammed. Rob's father had yelled at his mother to come back as the car tore out of the driveway. Rob had been terrified she'd smash into someone and kill them.

In the kitchen Rob had found puddles of booze and glass mixed in with smashed dinner plates and long splashes of whiskey sending drips down the yellow wall. He had fetched the broom and dustpan, intent on cleaning up the mess, and right away had sliced his finger on a shard of glass. It bled and bled. In the morning his mother had told him not to worry, his cut wasn't that bad; but without stitches it had taken weeks to heal.

Rob would always hate the long white scar running down his middle finger.

Chapter 10

"Are you getting ready?"

"I told you I'm not going."

"Of course you're going. Get out of those sweat pants. Now!"

Rob's father slammed Rob's room door shut. Rob dropped his magazine on the floor and stared at the ceiling. The grey daylight and the pelting of cold rain on the roof had made it easy to laze around on his bed reading karate magazines.

It wasn't that he minded going to Aunt Patty's for Thanksgiving dinner. What bothered him was that this was the first time *his* family wouldn't be together for turkey dinner. He didn't like the image of his father home alone. Besides, the Winnipeg Bombers were playing the Toronto Argonauts, and Rob and his Dad had always watched the Thanksgiving game together.

"Don't keep your aunt waiting, Rob. I'll be in the car."

Aunt Patty was his mother's youngest sister and her complete opposite – always cooking and cleaning and placing her husband and children first, never complaining.

They drove up in front of a newly built, large brick home. The front yard hadn't been landscaped yet and rain was turning it into a muddy plain.

Rob's dad gripped the steering wheel for a moment and looked ahead. "I'm sure you'll enjoy dinner. Your aunt's a great cook."

"Yeah, I know."

"Hopefully, your mother will behave herself."

"I don't even care about that."

Rob's dad understood the touch on his arm. "I'll be fine, Rob. Just go."

As Rob walked up, a black and white mutt on the front step started barking. Aunt Patty flung open the metal screen door, saying "Toby, quiet." But the dog jumped up on Rob and dirtied his dress pants.

"Bad Toby! Hi Rob, I'm so sorry," his aunt said, giving him a peck on the cheek.

Rob looked over at the dining room. It was set with the china, silver and crystal. Aunt Patty really knew how to make a nice dinner.

After he'd tidied himself up, Aunt Patty said, "Uncle Phil's in the rec room, why don't you keep him company?" Rob wandered down the stairs into the basement. It was finished in wood panelling and had a real bar.

"Sit down, young man," said Uncle Phil, who was watching the game. "Wanna Coke?"

"Sure." Rob took a chance. "Could I have some rum in it?"

Uncle Phil's belly shook. "Too early for that, young man."

Rob settled into the brown armchair. "What's the score?"

"Twenty-one nothing, the Argos. Most boring game I've ever seen – the Bombers can't get out of their end zone. Your father watching it?"

"Yup." Rob wished he were watching the game back home.

"What's keeping your mother?" said Uncle Phil, checking his watch. "I hope she's not planning to keep dinner waiting."

At 6:30 Rob's mother still hadn't arrived, but Uncle Phil turned off the TV anyway. Aunt Patty and the twins had started bringing out dinner. Rob said hello to Jennifer and Susan, who were sporting identical brown ponytails as usual. He didn't have much in common with them; they were only twelve.

Rob's uncle began slicing the turkey; the smell was irresistible. Rob looked longingly at the food – potatoes, thick gravy floating in a china bowl, cranberry sauce with whole berries swimming in it.

For a while the electric carving knife made conversation difficult. Finally the buzzing stopped. "Honey, where do you want the turkey?"

"There," said Aunt Patty, gesturing at a spot in the middle of the crowded table. She reached to light the candles, "I sure hope Sandra's on her way! Everything is ready."

"Where the Christ is your mother, Rob?" said Uncle Phil.

"I don't know. Do you want me to try calling her?" Rob said, staring into his plate.

"Don't worry, Rob," Aunt Patty said kindly, going into the kitchen. "I'll give her apartment a ring. But I'm sure she's on her way."

Uncle Phil looked impatient. "Well, we're all hungry. We might as well have some bread." He reached for the breadbasket and pulled out a big end before passing the basket to Rob. Rob grabbed a piece and gave the basket to his cousin Jennifer. He watched Uncle Phil plaster his bread with butter and swallow the massive piece in one bite.

"We might as well have some wine, too," said Uncle Phil, uncorking a bottle of red. He walked over to Aunt Patty's place and filled her glass halfway. Then he poured himself a full glass. "You want some, Rob?"

"I'll pass, thanks." Rob worried it might give his mother license to slosh it back if he was drinking too.

"Patty, should I pour your sister a glass?" he called into the kitchen.

She shouted, "Let's wait and see if she wants any."

What a joke, waiting to see *if*, thought Rob.

The doorbell rang and soon his mother came stumbling into the hallway, making a slurred apology. Rob couldn't believe she'd driven over in that condition.

Rob's uncle tried to help her off with her coat, catching the sleeve on her right hand. "Wait a minute, Phil. Christ!" she shouted. Struggling and yanking, she finally got free of the coat. "Hi, baby," she said, walking over to Rob, and bending down to kiss him. Her sugary breath made Rob pull back, so she grabbed his head and forced it towards her.

She plunked down in the empty chair. "Hey Phil, what's the madder, pour your guest some of that fine wine." He poured Mrs. Ethan half a glass. "Geez, Phil, don't be so goddamn stingy."

Rob cringed. He had hoped that once his mother had her wine she'd quiet down.

They began passing around the dishes. Rob filled his plate with turkey, potato, peas and stuffing and waited for everyone else to be served. But next Aunt Patty had an announcement. "Before we start eating, I want to pass on Uncle Tom's greetings to everyone, from Vancouver. He sends all of us his love and good wishes in the coming season."

"That bum, he never calls me," Mrs. Ethan muttered.

"Sandra, would you be a dear and pass the cranberries?"

Rob's mother reached unsteadily for the bowl. "Careful!" Uncle Phil yelled, but it was too late. Everyone watched the bowl slowly slide off the drip plate and land face down on the white embroidered tablecloth.

Rob's face went white. The red sauce had splattered everywhere, including his mother's dress and the twins' faces.

"What a godawful mess," said Uncle Phil, running to the kitchen.

Rob scooped the mound of cranberry sauce onto his side plate. When Uncle Phil returned with a stack of tea towels, Aunt Patty poured salt all over the large stain and began to scrub.

"God, Patty, I hope this isn't a good tablecloth," Rob's mom said.

"It was Phil's grandmother's."

Uncle Phil just stared down at the large oval stain on the tablecloth.

"Say, Patty, I bet you made one of your famous blueberry pies for dessert." This bright comment did not lighten the mood.

"That's right," Aunt Patty said tightly.

"Rob'll enjoy that, won't you, dear?"

"And imagine, it won't even matter if he slops it all over the tablecloth," said Uncle Phil.

As it turned out, Rob didn't have the chance. Dinner had run so late and that as dessert was coming out he heard – with relief – his father's car in the driveway. After a brief parting exchange with his aunt and uncle and an even briefer one with his mother, Rob tramped through the mud puddles to his father's car.

"So how was it?

"OK."

"How was she?"

"Oh, about average."

Chapter 11

Rob let out an early-morning yawn in the lineup at the lounge cafeteria. Ooo, there was Alana in the corner sipping a coffee with a book on her lap. He ordered a second honey-dip donut and made his way to the brown sofa across from her.

Alana looked up and smiled. "You're at school early this morning."

Rob felt an urge to smooth back his hair and fix his collar, but he was holding coffee and donuts. "Up and at 'em, my new philosophy in life. No more sleeping in late. By the way, I got you a donut."

"Yum, my favourite! What a nice bloke you are."

Rob grinned at her turn of phrase. "I see you're reading today's assignment. What's your position going to be for the term paper?"

"I'm definitely on the pro-punishment side. As far as I'm concerned, rehabilitation is a complete sham."

"You sound pretty hard-line."

"You have to put up with a lot of riffraff in England; there's been a horrid crime wave. My father's auto was pinched last year. So I believe in deterrence and a little vengeance thrown in for good measure."

"But you're ignoring a person's genetics and social background. You know, nature and nurture. If personalities are shaped by upbringing, rehabilitation is the best way to deal with criminals. We need to reshape their psychological makeup to conform with society's moral standards."

"Bull," answered Alana, making a thumbs-down sign. "The fact of the matter is, criminals choose between right or wrong. You choose to go to class or not, right? If criminals choose to commit a crime, they're responsible. We need to punish those who act voluntarily for their actions."

"Yeah, but what if I am so stoned or drunk I don't know what I'm doing? Say I'm so stoned that I microwave a baby instead of the turkey, then carve it up for Thanksgiving dinner. Is that free will?"

"*That* is totally repulsive!"

"I was just making a point." Rob flushed, regretting his example. He wanted everything he said to impress Alana.

"If you choose to take drugs or drink, that's voluntary, so you're responsible for your state of mind and should be punished."

"OK, what if I'm an alcoholic? What if the compulsion to drink is so bad that I just can't stop myself? Now, you can't punish someone for taking a first drink because they don't know that they are going to become an addict. It's due to their genes or their upbringing or both. If they lead to a crime committed while drunk, how is that person responsible?"

"Yes, but people beat their addiction all the time. So there must be free will. It's simply that the alcoholic doesn't want to stop or is just too lazy to try hard enough."

Rob's mother's face focused in his mind. He saw her behind the wheel, swerving all over the road and crashing. For a moment, his thoughts became scrambled and he lost confidence in his position.

In a subdued voice, Rob tried again. "Isn't treatment a more appropriate response then just throwing people in jail and turning them into worse creatures? If they get treatment for their addiction and beat it, why can't they rejoin society? Then they're not a threat to themselves or others."

"Well, to start with, the Bible says 'an eye for an eye and a tooth for a tooth.' If you commit a crime, you deserve to be punished. You've harmed society."

"OK, let's say I kill somebody and get life. I'm not the same person in ten years, am I? There are physical and psychological changes; my cells completely regenerate. My personality could change – say I became a born-again Christian. The person who committed the crime no longer exists. Why continue to punish someone who is not the same as the person who offended?"

"There is a need for deterrence, Rob. Your cellular theory is a load of crap," Alana said in her high-pitched English accent. "Even if a person has reformed, their punishment will deter others from committing the same crime, since they will know they're going to jail for life. The threat of punishment does deter people – otherwise, you'd steal a million bucks because you'd know there was no punishment attached to the act."

"I wouldn't if my moral values taught me it was wrong to steal. Punishment is a poor excuse for our society's failure to teach a moral distinction between right and wrong. Some of us have had terrible upbringings and lousy role models."

Rob's mouth shut tight; his face went deep red. Alana sat back in her armchair, observing, and took a sip of coffee.

"What I'm trying to say is," Rob murmured, "if deterrence is used as a means to an end, why not use medieval justice and cut off a thief's hand for stealing? Why not inflict horrible torture that would really deter people? The crime rate would plummet."

"Certainly, but you have to temper the need for justice with the assurance that the punishment fits the crime. Otherwise, people will lose respect for the system. If they know they are going to lose a hand for shoplifting, they'll figure they might as well rob a bank. That theory doesn't hold water, Rob."

"So they lose both hands for robbing a bank and a lot more for rape," Rob grinned.

Alana's hard expression softened with a smile and she looked at her watch. "Let's agree to disagree, alright? Time for class, my wise friend."

Chapter 12

"I called her!"

"Did she say yes?"

"She wasn't home yet, so I left a message for her to phone me."

"What movie you taking her to?" Julius asked.

"*Jaws.* She hasn't seen it yet."

"Great, she'll be grabbing you all night long."

"I don't need a movie to get her to do that."

"What a badass!"

"Listen, I gotta go. It's almost five, she'll be home soon."

Rob fished around in the cookie bag on the kitchen table – only broken pieces left. A deep gulp of milk quenched his thirst. He rested his feet on the other chair and waited for the phone call.

Alana and Rob had been meeting in the lounge for coffee every day. School and music were the main topics. But yesterday she had teased him about his new haircut, short and layered. She said it accented his refined nose and large blue eyes.

The phone startled him.

"Hello!" he said expectantly.

"Rob, your mother's been in an accident," said a man's quivering voice.

"Dad, what?"

"I'm at the hospital. Uncle Phil's on his way to pick you up." Rob hung up and stood frozen as his heartbeat skyrocketed.

He yanked his coat from the closet and left the hanger where it clattered to the floor. As he waited in the armchair by the front door, snapshots of freedom from his mother's problems danced in his mind. Life would be so simple if she died.

Headlights wheeled into the driveway. There were Uncle Phil and Aunt Patty, the worry showing on their faces. Rob slid into the back seat of the black Buick.

Aunt Patty held on to the scarf covering her curlers as the Buick lurched out of the driveway and sped down the street. "Any news from your Dad?" she asked, turning towards Rob with tears in her eyes.

"No, he didn't call back."

"I wouldn't worry. That woman has nine lives," said Uncle Phil.

"Sure, but maybe they've all been used," Rob answered.

Rob and Aunt Patty watched silently as Uncle Phil wove through the traffic, pushing beyond the speed limit in the clear sections, until the car jolted to a stop in the hospital parking lot. The emergency entrance was brightened by the blinking red lights of an ambulance.

Every green vinyl chair was filled with some relative or friend waiting for news. Mr. Ethan motioned them to the hallway near the intake desk. He looked grim, and Rob stood soldier-like as his father hugged him.

"Sandra's inside. They don't know much yet." His hands shook as he took the coffee Uncle Phil held out to him.

"She'll be OK," Rob said, controlling his emotions.

Aunt Patty blotted her eyes. "What happened?"

"Supposedly she was driving down Bishop and lost control. She hit a tree in the median. The car was so badly crushed they had to cut her out."

"What kind of injuries?" Aunt Patty said in a quivery voice.

"A serious cut from hitting the windshield, legs pretty bad and they don't know what's going on internally. The x-rays will show them."

Rob's stomach fluttered as a police officer approached the group. "Who's the next of kin?"

Rob's father stood up. "I'm her husband, but we're separated. This is her sister," he said, pointing at Aunt Patty.

"I'll talk to you both. Let's go over there." Rob's dad put his arm around Aunt Patty and escorted her to the far corner of the waiting room. After a few minutes of questions and answers in both directions, they shook the officer's hand and came back towards Rob and his uncle.

"She was drinking," Aunt Patty blurted.

"Hell, of course she was," Uncle Phil said scornfully. "Why else would she drive off the road and hit a tree in the middle of the boulevard?"

His aunt hesitated and glanced at Rob's father. "Tell them, Patty."

"The police officer found an envelope from her work on the front seat..." Aunt Patty started to gasp.

"It's OK, take a breath," said Mr. Ethan. The colour drained out of Rob's face.

"She was fired for missing work and showing up late. All those years down the drain. I don't understand."

Rob crossed his arms and leaned against the wall.

"Christ, so she went and tried to kill herself," said Uncle Phil.

"Phil, you don't know that," scolded Mr. Ethan.

Rob drifted off to a chair. He imagined his mother steering straight at a tree and the crushing impact. Had she fallen asleep at the wheel? Or had she felt a split-second impulse to end her misery? He wished he knew.

As the second hand on the wall crept round and round, the chatter of his family drifted away and Rob slipped into a childhood memory. His mother was driving slowly, weaving across the centre line and pulling back into her lane whenever a car came towards them. Rob had pled with her to be more careful, but she had only warned him to stop pestering her. As she turned off to their house, he had seen a semi-trailer coming at them. He had yanked the steering wheel and yelled; the truck barrelled by, too close.

"Charles Ethan and Patty Newman," a nurse called out. Rob picked up a crumpled Time magazine, relieved he didn't have to see his mother.

"You're mother's going to be in hock for that car, you know." Uncle Phil had come to sit by him. "The insurance company won't pay for it because she was drunk."

"How do you know that?"

"Believe me, that's what happens."

Rob recalled how he'd spoken in favour of his mother when she'd asked his father to co-sign her loan. Another stupid mistake – now his father was going to be out the money for the car.

Mr. Ethan appeared through the double doors and came to sit on the other side of Rob. "They think she'll probably make it, Rob, but it's touch and go. She might need surgery for the head injury and the broken leg." He straightened his collar with a shaky hand.

Rob swallowed. "Did the cop say she'd be charged?"

"Depends on her blood alcohol level at the time of impact."

A nurse with red hair and freckles came up to Rob and his father. "You can see Mrs. Ethan, but you should know there's some swelling."

They followed the nurse into the ICU. Rob could hardly tell which patient was his mother. The top of Mrs. Ethan's head was wrapped in bandages and the right side of her face was swollen like a balloon. Tubes ran into her throat and arm. The heart monitor blipped. She was barely conscious.

Rob stood back from the bed. Mr. Ethan touched her hand; when his wife opened her eyes they pooled with wordless tears.

The next day, Rob and his dad returned to the hospital. A few minutes after they'd announced themselves to the waiting room receptionist, a young doctor in surgical greens approached. Beads of sweat dotted his forehead.

"Hi, I'm Dr. Kravchuck. Mr. Ethan, we're looking at surgery to remove a small amount of fluid from Mrs. Ethan's brain. Let me explain to you about brain trauma. When the brain has been injured it swells and fluid collects. If it swells too much, it presses against the skull and this can be quite serious. So we have to try to prevent swelling and ensure proper blood flow to the brain."

Doesn't sound that bad, thought Rob, pushing fear from his mind.

"But it's good news that she's conscious and that she can hear."

See? She'll be fine, thought Rob. He was pleased that he didn't feel worried.

That evening, after his mother's surgery, Rob and his father joined Aunt Patty in a visit to the recovery ward. A dozen beds were lined up on opposite sides of the room; again they had to look around to find Rob's mother. Now her head was wrapped in white gauze and the side of her face had turned from red to black.

Mrs. Ethan blinked when the trio approached. She looked at Rob, but he stood back from the bed. It was difficult to move; his feet felt glued to the floor. "Say something to her," Mr. Ethan said, pushing Rob closer.

"Glad you're OK. You should be back to your old self soon."

But then he worried she think he was being sarcastic? "You know what I mean – soon you'll be up and around." No other words came to him, so he stepped away from the bed.

The bandages brought back a memory of when he was ten and he had been briefly left alone one evening. He'd been lighting pieces of paper towel on the counter. The flames gave him a thrill, so he had made a big ball of paper and lit it. The resulting fireball had scared him; he had tried to push it into the sink, but it had fallen off the counter onto his foot. The fire had burnt itself out, but Rob had a large red welt on his foot that stung like hell.

When his mother came home from the store with cigarettes and a brown booze bag, she had immediately asked about the smoke smell. Rob at first had said he knew nothing, but then the burn hurt more and more and a large watery blister was growing on top of the foot. Tears of pain and shame had burst from his eyes. He had wanted forgiveness and sympathy.

Instead, Rob's mother had dragged him by the arm to his bedroom, letting his injured foot skid down the carpet in the hall. As he screamed from fear and intense hurt his mother had pulled his jeans down and strapped him with a leather belt, telling him how bad he was and how he had nearly burned the house down.

Later that evening his mother had wrapped his foot in soft gauze and applied a soothing ointment. As she cut the tape from the dressing, he was so angry he had hit her. After she was finished with him, he had learned not to get angry with her ever again.

Chapter 13

For several days Rob spent hours with his father and aunt in the hospital. He thought a lot about life and death. It was weird how life could swing in any direction and you couldn't see what was coming.

Once Aunt Patty asked, "How's school going?"

"Great!" He felt a pang of guilt for this white lie. School had been going OK, but he hadn't opened a book since the accident.

Dr. Kravchuck approached, removing the mask tied around his neck. "She's very lucky. The surgery relieved the immediate pressure and now the swelling is reduced considerably, so the pressure is staying down where it belongs."

Before they could feel too relieved, he went on.

"But it's not all over; her right leg will be in a cast for three to four months. Hopefully, there aren't too many stairs at home for her to navigate," the doctor said with a grin.

Rob's father cleared his voice and said, "Mrs. Ethan and I are not living together, doctor. I'm not sure where she's going to be living."

The young intern flushed. "You'll need to make arrangements for someone to care for her."

"She'll be staying with me, doctor," Aunt Patty said softly. "I'll be taking care of her."

Rob's father touched Aunt Patty on the arm and she gave him

a little smile.

"You can go in to visit now," said Dr. Kravchuck. "If you have any more questions, catch me on the ward."

"Did you ask Phil?" Mr. Ethan asked Aunt Patty.

"No, but he'll be fine. I'll put her down in the basement."

Yeah, a dungeon's about right for her, thought Rob.

"We'll pack up everything in her apartment on the weekend," Mr. Ethan said, looking at Rob.

That'll be a rotten job, Rob thought. But at least he wouldn't have to visit her in that horrible place again.

A grey-haired nurse guided the family to Mrs. Ethan's hospital room. "The pain medication is making her groggy, but she sure has come along since the surgery."

"We'll be brief," Rob's father said.

They entered a room with two other sleeping people. Aunt Patty whispered, "Hello, Sandra, you look much better," squeezing her sister's hand.

"I don't feel better," Mrs. Ethan said in a husky voice – but she had hardly talked at all on their previous visits.

"The doctor said you'll be able to leave in a week."

"For me, this place is the Hilton. I'm in no hurry," she said cynically. She turned her head towards Rob. "You're looking thin."

"I'm OK. You seem better," Rob whispered.

"Well, I'm alive and I'm sober," his mother chuckled. "I'll bet you're all happy about that."

"We want you to get your life sorted out. You know that," Rob's father said. He reached to touch her arm but then put his hand down.

"I know I've been a pain. Maybe I do need help – imagine me saying that!"

"You know I'll be there to help you when you get out of hospital," Aunt Patty said, giving her a hug.

"But that's not the only help you need, Sandra. You know that," said Mr. Ethan.

Rob wondered what he meant.

When they left the hospital room, a well-dressed man and woman were waiting outside the door. Rob assumed they were visiting one of the other patients in the room. But Mr. Ethan went up to them. "Bud, Jeannie, thanks for coming. By the way, this is my son, Rob."

Bud was a short older man with dyed-black hair. During their handshake, a chunky gold bracelet slapped against Rob's hand. He must be rich, thought Rob.

"Pleasure to meet you, Rob," said Bud, squeezing his hand and looking him in the eye. "Your mother has spoken of you many a time."

"Nice to meet you, too," Rob answered. How did this couple know his mother?

Jeannie was as short as Bud. "How do you do, Rob?" she said, giving him a gentle hug. Her head of grey curls only came up to Rob's chin.

"I heard you're a university student," offered Bud. "Studying philosophy! That'll get you thinking."

"I guess."

"Figured out the meaning of life, yet?"

"Not yet, actually. I probably won't before Christmas."

Bud gave a spirited laugh. "No worries, I've been working on it for fifty years. You have lots of time."

"Hope it gets easier."

"It's never easy, son, though sometimes you see the path a little clearer."

"Good, 'cause I seem to get lost more often than most people," said Rob, looking at his feet.

"I know," said Bud. "I have confidence in you." Rob wondered how Bud knew so much about him.

"Well, Jeannie, we'd better go in and see how the patient is." They moved towards the hospital room door. "Nice to meet you, Rob. We'll cross paths again." He shook Rob's hand and patted his back.

Rob felt the warm touch. He asked himself, who *are* these people?

Saturday Rob and his dad started early, driving a small rented truck to the North End. Dishes with hardened food were stacked in the sink. Empty Scotch bottles were lined up by the kitchen garbage can and plastic cups were scattered everywhere. The fig tree had turned yellow. The fridge held mouldy macaroni and cheese, a bag of rotten peaches and little else.

"Why don't we start on the kitchen," said Mr. Ethan.

"I can't wait!"

They gingerly plucked out the decayed food and threw it into a garbage bag. Then they washed the dishes and packed them up.

Next they moved over to the bed area in the one-room apartment. His father started packing up the clothes in his mother's dresser. "Why don't you do her night table?"

Rob carefully wrapped all of his mother's junky knickknacks. "Where did she get all this stuff?"

"At bingo," Rob's father said, chuckling.

Rob opened the top drawer. It was full of photos of himself as a child. Picking up the photographs one by one, Rob tried to remember the ages when they were taken. In some of them he was acting in school plays as a cowboy, a tree. Several others showed a young boy gleefully unwrapping his Christmas presents.

At the drawer's bottom lay a shiny metal object – it was the first medal Rob had ever won in a karate tournament. He stuffed it into his jeans, wondering why his mother would have taken it.

The bottom drawer held only some packages of Kleenex and a book covered with aluminum foil wrap. Rob opened the cover and saw a name handwritten in pencil on the inside cover – Jeannie Lawton. He sat down on the bed and flipped through a few pages.

"We have to take the sofa and bed down," his father called. "You done packing?"

"Almost. Where should I put the garbage?"

"The bin behind the building. What are you doing with that book?"

"I want to hang on to it for mom," he said, grabbing the black garbage bag while he gripped the book under his arm.

Aunt Patty gave them lunch. They got the truck partly unloaded before Rob had to go to karate. "I can finish this up," Rob's dad said. "Six o'clock at the Tung Hing?"

The Chinese restaurant meal was Rob's payment for helping with the moving. Rob was so hungry he ploughed down three servings. As he was emptying the chow mein bowl onto his plate, he asked his father the question he'd been wondering about for three days.

"Who were those people at the hospital? You know, the other day?"

"You mean Bud and Jeannie? Bud is your Uncle Ralph's AA sponsor." Ralph was Mr. Ethan's brother. When Rob was a child he'd known Uncle Ralph as a rowdy, beer-drinking guy who didn't seem to ever go to work. But since Ralph had become sober seven years ago he'd built a successful plumbing business and moved into the wealthy part of town.

"A few months before she left home Uncle Ralph introduced Jeannie to your mom. She helped your mom through some rough times. But Jeannie let her go when she didn't stick with the program."

The waitress arrived with the bill and fortune cookies. Mr. Ethan gestured at the cookies. "You go first."

Rob picked up a cookie and cracked it open.

"What's it say?"

Rob swallowed. "A lifetime of happiness lies ahead of you."

"Hey, nice fortune," said Mr. Ethan. "Hope it comes true. Better than mine."

"What's yours say?"

"Never trouble trouble till trouble troubles you."

"Huh? Say that again."

Chapter 14

Rob raced up to the second floor and kicked off his shoes, placing them beside the other pairs already lined up neatly against the wall.

Now in the large, airy dojo room, he dropped to his knees on the wooden floor, leaning forward until his forehead rested on his hands.

Having completed the bow, he entered the dressing room. He pulled on his white gi pants, tying the waist string snugly. He tied the gi top by strings on each side to keep it closed. Then he dug through into his duffle bag and pulled out the brown belt. He wrapped it around his waist twice, knotting it in front of his stomach in the correct fashion. He checked his image in the large mirror. OK.

He walked back to the door of the dojo room and bowed again. The other students chatted, but Rob stood alone, trying to build confidence for the class ahead. The head instructor, Sensei Matt Sonberg appeared from the small office, nodding at Rob as he moved to the front of the class to take command.

The Sensei was a tall, thick man with a trim beard and a serious face. The legend around the dojo was that Sensei had been a Marine and had seen heavy combat in Vietnam. Rob didn't know that for sure, though he did know that Sensei was a prison guard in his day job.

"Line up, gentlemen, are you ready for a little burn tonight?" Sensei pushed up his gi sleeves, exposing tattoos. The positioning of the class went from the highest belt at the front to the lower ranks at the back. Rob took his place in the front line of the class.

"*Sanchin kata!*"

The class moved in unison to begin the *kata* form.

"Ready position."

The students moved together to the first position and stood motionless with their right legs forward and their arms bent in front of their chests.

"Excellent. This *kata* will condition your body against pain and mind against fear. Learn to resolve the three conflicts, mind, body and spirit. All should be one when performing *Sanchin kata.*"

It was time for Sensei to test each *karateka's* stance, focus and conditioning, beginning at the right end of the front row. Sensei knew exactly how much power to deliver without causing injury.

Terry Wilson, the senior student in the class, came first. Rob thought he was a show-off and didn't care for him much. Sensei moved in front of Wilson and delivered a punch to his midsection. There were two thuds, as Wilson gasped for breath and a blow knocked him back.

He should have breathed out sooner, Rob thought to himself.

After a few minutes the Sensei came to Rob. He pushed gently on Rob's hip to check whether he would sway back and lose his stance. He pushed down on Rob's arms to see if Rob could let them spring into his body and out. He walked behind Rob and jabbed his knuckles into the back muscles, to test if Rob was pulling down his shoulders. Then he hit Rob's lower back with open palms, causing Rob to move forward a few inches.

Fighting to regain his stance, Rob grabbed the floor with his toes and screwed his heels together. He stared into space, trying to have no thoughts, fears or anticipations.

Sensei placed his foot on the back of Rob's calf muscle and pushed it forward. The leg gave way slightly, but Rob struggled to keep his heel from lifting. Then Sensei came around and kicked the front of Rob's thigh. It burned, but not sharply. He touched his fist on Rob's stomach, then wound up and struck. Rob absorbed the power by softening the inside of the stomach wall.

"Get your breathing down."

The next strike was harder. Rob hadn't been ready, and it winded him. He lurched backwards and gasped for air.

"Tuck up, pull your heels together," said Sensei.

Rob shook his head and tried to refocus.

Sensei flicked his fingers at Rob's eyes, coming within a hair's width of his eyeballs. Rob blinked but did not move his head. Moving to the rear, he put one finger on the top of Rob's shoulder and pulled him gently back. Rob felt his body start to tumble backwards like a falling board. His feet were not screwed into the floor with enough strength to pass this test.

As Sensei went on to the next student, Rob berated himself. He thought, I should've done that last one better; I always mess up. There were more thuds as the teacher's hands and feet met their targets until finally the testing was over.

"Slow speed," Sensei Sonberg commanded. The students began moving through the form. Rob fought to keep his shoulders down as each arm thrust out at his imaginary assailant's chest. With each step he tried to screw his feet into the floor to become rooted. This was how stability and power were generated, Sensei had said; the steps had to be stealthy and tigerlike.

"Again, *Sanchin kata.* You have to empty your mind to enter *mushin,* natural consciousness. When you're attacked on the street, you don't have time to debate which block or counterstrike to use. You have to be governed by instinct and calmness. *Mushin* is what lets your body react instantly and counterstrike without thought. Bring this into your *kata.*"

The rows of students bowed their heads to Sensei with perfect timing and began the basic *kata* a final time.

At the end of the class, Rob walked back to the changing room comparing his performance to that of the best students. He was sure he would never make it up to their level, no matter how hard he tried.

Chapter 15

"Rob, you busy?"

"No, what's up?" Rob was finishing dinner. His dad was working late that evening, so Rob was just having a late-evening sandwich instead of supper.

"I gotta get out of here, I'll come over."

"OK. Come to the back door."

In a few minutes Julius was standing on the back stoop in the rain in only a tie-dye sweatshirt and jeans.

"Come in, man. You're getting soaked."

"You wanna come out and get stoned?" Julius said rapidly, the rain drenching his hair. "I just blew a fat one – good shit, man."

"No thanks." He hoped Julius didn't have his drugs with him. "You coming in?"

Julius came in and sat down on the kitchen chair, wiping the dripping water from his forehead. His eyes were glassy.

"Are you OK?" asked Rob.

"I had a fight with my old man; he said fifty bucks was missing from his wallet. But I didn't take it. Christ, anyone could've lifted it; he was out getting sloshed."

"Maybe your father pissed it away at a bar." In truth, Rob wondered where Julius got money to buy drugs.

"He does love being a hero, buying rounds for his buddies." Julius slouched into the kitchen chair and looked out the window. His face looked especially gaunt.

"You missed every class this week. You sick?"

"No, just bagged. Slept in."

"I've been bagged too. Spending all that time in that creepy hospital. Man, there are some pretty gross people in there." Rob looked at his empty glass, wishing there was another bottle of Coke in the fridge. His dad never bought enough.

Julius poured himself the last bit of Coke in the bottle and said, "When's your old lady getting out, anyways?"

"Probably in a few days."

"Will she get charged?"

"Not sure."

"If she does, she'll lose her license for six months. Oh yeah, and have to pay $500. That's what happened to my old man – though that might've been his second time."

That would be a lot of money, Rob thought, on top of paying off the loan on the wrecked car. He got up and dumped his ice cubes in the sink.

"Don't worry, they'll give her time to pay," Julius added.

"Yeah, but she lost her job."

"So she'll do jail time instead."

Rob didn't like the picture of his own mother locked up in jail and had a fearful vision of running into Sensei Sonberg when he went to visit her. "Maybe my aunt can lend her some money."

"Got any chips?" asked Julius. "I've got the munchies bad."

The key turned in the back door lock and Mr. Ethan entered. "Hi Rob. It's nasty out there." He shook water off his coat and hung it up.

Rob looked nervously between Julius and his father. "This is Julius, he's in my philosophy class."

Mr. Ethan scanned Julius' long hair and blank face, sizing him up. "I'll fix a sandwich and then be out of your way."

Julius looked fidgety. Maybe Dad knows he's stoned, thought Rob. "I think I'll head out. Want to go to McDonalds, Rob?"

"No, the weather is too crappy. And I've got an early karate class tomorrow."

"Then see you later, dude. Thanks for the Coke." He disappeared into the rain.

Rob's father sat in the chair Julius had occupied.

"Who's this new friend?" Mr. Ethan said sternly. "He looks like a druggie. Is he?"

"Not sure."

"You know to stay away from that stuff, right?"

"Right."

Rob's father stood. "Well, then, I'm off to bed."

"Me too. Goodnight, Dad."

When Rob went into his room, he noticed his father had done laundry for him and taken care to fold his karate uniform neatly on the bed.

The window rattled and roof creaked. Rob was pleased he hadn't headed into the storm with Julius. When he reached from under the covers to turn out the light, he saw Jeannie Lawton's book with the tinfoil cover wrap on his night table and turned to the title page:

Alcoholics Anonymous: The Story of How Many Thousands of Men and Women Have Recovered from Alcoholism
Third Edition
Alcoholics Anonymous World Services Inc.
New York City

Was his mother a real alcoholic? Rob wondered. Before the

separation, she'd always stayed out of serious trouble and held down a job. Three years ago she'd even won a curling club championship. It was only lately that she'd started drinking all of the time, hanging around bars and finally crashing her car.

He leafed through the book some more, stopping on a list of twelve steps in bold letters. The first step read:

"1. We admitted we were powerless over alcohol – that our lives had become unmanageable."

Rob reread the words three times, thinking about who they fit. Certainly his mother's life was a disaster. Julius also came to mind. But his own life did not exactly seem under control, either. Life in his family was like being in the middle of a blizzard, he thought, wind gusting in all directions. You can't see where you're heading, and as soon as you clear away one hill of snow another blows in on you. No one can control a storm. Does that mean you have to surrender to its power?

Rob looked down at the book again and read another step.

"2. Came to believe that a Power greater than ourselves could restore us to sanity."

This one didn't make sense to him, the way the first step had. It seemed to be saying you had to call on God to fix your life. But he'd realized in philosophy class that he didn't believe in a God who meddled around in people's lives, making everything OK. God didn't control the chaos in the world. Rob thought himself an atheist.

No, he wasn't going to be able to do number two. Maybe this book wasn't going to be as useful as he'd first thought.

Chapter 16

"Last *kata* for this morning is *Seisan kata* at test speed. Begin!"

Seisan kata was thirteen complicated defensive blocking and counterstrike moves. Sensei stepped back to assess the class, paying particular attention to the brown belt students in the front row.

Rob had to perfect this form to earn his black belt. Aware of Sensei's gaze, he executed the form at full speed.

"Sit!"

As the class dropped to the floor, most of them panted for air. Sensei rubbed his palms together to indicate he was not pleased with the class performance. "It's not a race," he criticized, pounding his fist into his open palm. "Don't rush the moves."

Then, in a calmer voice, he said, "You must be fully present when you do your *kata*. It's no different from how you should be in life. Don't dwell on the last move. Don't think about the moves coming up until you've finished the one you're on."

Turning to one of the students who was still winded, he said, "Ricky, you're panting like a dog. You have to breathe in the *kata!*"

He turned to the whole class. "After you complete each strike, step and breathe. Savour the air in your lungs. But don't fill up like a balloon – draw a half breath and push it down into your stomach. Then push out your stomach and force some air up and out your mouth. And concentrate on keeping your breathing low in your body below your belly button – that's where your power comes from."

Sensei Sonberg drew his arm back and thrust, rotating his hips towards the target. The floor vibrated from the power of his strike. "Don't use your upper body to strike," he instructed. "Move your legs and hips with the strike to deliver power from your stance. Then let the arm shoot out like an arrow from a bow."

Rob watched and tried to absorb everything Sensei said. There were so many things you had to co-ordinate at the same time when you were doing a *kata.*

"Now, twenty minutes of sparring," Sensei ordered.

Rob felt a rush of adrenaline quicken his breath. He anxiously fumbled through his bag to find his sparring gear and went back to his spot on the floor.

Turning to his right, he bowed to his opponent, Dave Friesen. He was a huge guy with glasses.

"I'm tired already, man," he said to Rob. "Let's go easy."

The two touched gloves. Dave inched towards Rob, sending a right punch and a front kick. But the blows missed and Rob moved back out of range. The hefty guy charged in again. Surprised by his timing, Rob didn't move fast enough, and a right bounced off his left shoulder and smacked his jaw.

Dave followed up with another right to his side. The pain to his ribs was instant. Rob dropped his arm and signalled that he needed a break. Dave wiped off his foggy glasses on his gi.

After a few seconds it was time to go again. They touched gloves. This time, when Dave lunged forward, Rob counterpunched as soon as he saw his opponent move and caught him with a hard right to the belly. The soft target gave way and Dave buckled.

Then Dave counterattacked ferociously. Arms and legs flew at Rob until he retreated. He put up his arms; he felt too overwhelmed by Dave's rage to fight back.

Sensei Sonberg ended the sparring session. "Bow to your partners. We'll do more work on this next time. You all have to learn to attack the attack and finish off your opponent with one technique," he lectured.

The students lined up and dropped to their knees to make a formal bow. The room reverberated as they performed a perfectly-timed clap. "*Domo Sensei!*" they yelled in unison to honour their instructor.

Sensei Sonberg bowed to them. "Remember, the sign-up sheets for the tournament are at the front desk. They have to be in by the end of November."

"Rob, are you going?" asked Dave.

"I haven't decided."

"Good class, man."

"Yeah, you too."

On the bus ride home, Rob touched his ribs; something didn't feel right. What about the upcoming tournament? Did he want to get his butt kicked around the ring by the best students in the city? He could imagine humiliation and discomfort.

But wait – he was worrying about a tournament he might or might not be in – fretting about the future, doing what Sensei had told them not to do.

A red bump was starting to come up on his hand, so he pressed his thumb into it. Now that was real. It was pain, and it was in the moment.

He thought about what Sensei had said about air and took a deep breath. There was a saying that you should live each day as if it were your last. Maybe we should also take every breath as if it were our last. Rob took another breath and filled his lungs. He let it out. That was powerful.

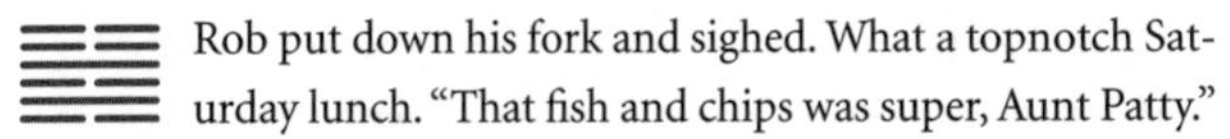

Chapter 17

Rob put down his fork and sighed. What a topnotch Saturday lunch. "That fish and chips was super, Aunt Patty."

Aunt Patty picked up his plate. "It was no trouble, kiddo. I'll go take care of the dishes and let you and your mom chat."

"Do you mind if Rob and I have a coffee in the living room?" Mrs. Ethan asked.

"Of course not!"

Rob helped his mother prop her leg up on some pillows on the couch and sat himself on a plump armchair. Mrs. Ethan lit a cigarette and blew smoke towards the ceiling. She looks nice this way, Rob thought, without her makeup. The dark bruise on the right side of her face had faded and her hair fell smoothly past her shoulders.

Blowing a smoke ring, she said, "So I've been hitting the bottom pretty much lately, huh honey?"

Rob looked out the window behind her. "How long are you going to be in the cast?"

"Maybe two months, maybe more. Sorry for all this crap, I'm not sure how you dealt with it all, especially when I was in the hospital, huh?"

Rob veered away from her topic. "Yeah, and then those people showed up."

"You mean Bud and Jeannie?"

"Yeah. Dad said Bud was Uncle Ralph's AA sponsor." Rob hoped she would ask about her book.

"Your uncle's done pretty well with his big house and all, huh?" She stubbed out her cigarette.

"Well, Mom, so can you!" There, he'd said it!

His mother looked away, but Rob saw tears in her eyes.

"If I had a life, maybe I wouldn't drink," she said, looking out the window.

"What do you mean? You had a life but you drank anyway – especially when we were a family," Rob said sharply.

"You're right, honey. It's me that's the problem," she said, breaking into sobs. "I have to accept that."

Rob's spirits lifted with her words. They sounded like the first step from the book.

"I know I've been a bad mother," she said in a weepy voice, resting the uninjured side of her face in her hand. "You don't deserve to have my problems in your life just when you're starting university. This should be a happy time for you."

This was the first time Rob could remember her saying anything about his happiness; he was used to her crying about her own problems.

"Don't worry about me," he stammered, disconcerted. "You gotta get your life straightened out."

"Chocolate chip cookies right out of the oven?"

Rob and his mother stared at Aunt Patty blankly, and when Aunt Patty saw her sister's teary face she retreated. "Maybe I'll put on some coffee," she said over her shoulder.

Mrs. Ethan lit another cigarette and looked out the window. "I know if I don't get help, I'm going to die."

"I'd say."

Suddenly she stamped out her cigarette and smiled bravely.

"Rob, I'm going to start now. No more drinking."

Rob didn't trust her yet. "You want your book?"

"What book?"

"The one Jeannie gave you. I took it from your apartment."

"Did you read it?" she asked with interest.

"Some."

"Maybe you should keep it for a while. I can always get another one."

Rob didn't like that. If she were really serious, wouldn't she have taken the book?

He gave her one more chance to prove herself. "Are you really going to try?"

Mrs. Ethan reached to touch her son's hand. "Promise."

A shiver raced up Rob's spine.

Chapter 18

Rob had been at Aunt Patty's longer than he'd planned. He left in a rush and within an hour he was running from the bus to the dojo, weaving between pedestrians in pouring rain.

By the time he reached the dojo he was out of breath and soaking wet. "You'd better move your ass or Sensei will be pissed," said Billy Thomas in the changing room, grinning as he feigned a kick. Billy was a cocky, heavy-set eighteen-year-old from the North End who'd had more than his share of street-corner fights.

Rob rushed into the change room. He slid on his protective cup and quickly positioned it, then he pulled on his damp gi pants. He had forgotten to put them in the dryer. His gi jacket felt even worse.

After ten minutes of warm-up exercise, Sensei told the students to get their sparring gear. "Let's get some practice in before the tournament," Sensei said, moving to the front to observe the action.

Rob's heart beat fast as he anticipated the fighting. He pulled on his fighting gloves, which were smaller than boxing gloves and covered only the tops of his hands; the fingers were open so you could grab your opponent. He fitted his mouth guard between his teeth.

Sensei demonstrated a practice combination. While the attacker threw a right punch, his opponent would block his chest with a *hirate mawashi uke,* a circular block that swept in front of the body.

"If you whip your block around you can deflect a heavy punch with minimal effort," Sensei explained. "Bring the arm right back to *Sanchin* position and counter with a roundhouse kick to the thigh," he added, demonstrating the kick.

Rob found himself matched up with Billy, who was shorter than he but twenty-five pounds heavier. By comparison, Rob's last partner Dave Friesen had been a marshmallow. Rob threw a punch at Billy's chest and Billy whipped his block around, knocking Rob's arm out of its intended path, and sent a heavy thud to the side of his thigh.

After they had alternated the two positions ten times, Rob could hardly stand up because of the pain on the side of his leg. Each kick jolted the same nerve. But he pushed himself through the agony until the exercise ended.

"Enough of that, boys," said Sensei. "Now start sparring."

Rob and Billy touched gloves and took a fighting stance. As soon as Rob met Billy's eyes and saw that cold, penetrating stare, his confidence sank.

Instantly, Billy darted in with a quick left and a right front kick to Rob's stomach. Rob retreated successfully, but Billy's quick aggression threw off his focus. The two circled, and Billy fired the same left hand and kick at Rob. Again, Rob moved back to set up for the next attack.

Sensei bellowed at him, "Rob, don't retreat! Attack his attack!"

Rob felt humiliated, but the words got his blood going.

Billy threw a roundhouse kick to Rob's thigh and came in with a straight right, as they'd been practising. This time, Rob deflected it with an open wrist block across his front.

"Good block, Rob," Sensei yelled. "But counterstrike immediately, when he's still off balance from his attack."

Rob nodded at Sensei. He knew all his effort was going into defence and that he had to be more aggressive. The problem was that he'd feel aggressive urges but wouldn't be able to let them loose to launch his attack and his power would evaporate.

This time Billy got nasty. He moved in and grabbed Rob's gi at the shoulder, digging in his fingers and pinching Rob's skin hard. Then, when Rob was distracted, he tried to hit Rob in the upper chest with a right.

Suddenly Rob responded; the searing pain from the grab had brought him to life. He broke Billy's grab by slicing his hand across his front. As Billy threw a left at Rob's head he anticipated it, moving his head to the right and catching Billy hard in the ribs with a roundhouse kick.

As Billy winced and covered his side with his left arm, Rob felt great. He'd finally scored!

But Rob's glee quickly turned to fear. In retaliation, Billy launched a flurry of hard, wild punches. Rob blocked most of them but a few landed.

When the two opponents faced each other again Rob sensed Billy's fierce spirit. Billy launched a right punch and then lifted his rear leg, intending it for Rob's midsection. Instinctively, Rob used his front shin to shield the attack so that Billy's toes smashed the bottom of Rob's knee – a classic crane block.

As Billy began hopping on his other foot to diffuse the pain, Sensei ordered all of the students to bow to each other.

The class sat in a circle around Sensei. "Too much reliance on the upper body is weak," he instructed. "You need to use your stance to add chi to your punches." He drew back his arm and thrust it out from his side like an arrow, so the floor vibrated from the tension remaining in his body.

"Chi is life energy, and though all living beings have it, it has to be cultivated and harnessed. In humans it's centred about an inch and a half below the belly button, in an area called the *dan tian*. One way to build chi is to use breathing techniques to stimulate the *dan tian*," Sensei explained.

"By forcing air down towards the belly, and then by pushing the breath out of the lower belly with one's stomach muscles, we can build a reservoir of chi and use it to strike an opponent very hard. Like the dragon, we have power in our breath."

As the students returned to their positions and bowed to Sensei, Rob concentrated on making every movement come from his lower body and keeping his upper body out of the action. He became aware of how each breath brought new strength.

Chapter 19

The room was dark and his father was calling his name. What was going on? This was Sunday morning, sleep-in time. When he entered the kitchen, his mother was sitting at the table smoking a cigarette.

"What are you doing here, Mom? Are you here to see Dad?" Rob asked hopefully. Was she there to try to work things out with his father?

"No, I'm going to do some work. You two can chat." And Mr. Ethan headed to the basement.

"It's you I wanted to see, honey," she said, gesturing him to a chair. "Sit down, for goodness' sake. You got me thinking yesterday when we were at Aunt Patty's."

She took a drag from the cigarette then tossed her hair back over one shoulder. "I want to tell you I'm sorry for everything that happened when you were a kid, and I'm trying to get my life together. I want to live sober."

Rob's mind reeled, but he kept his distance. "That sounds great, Mom. I'm happy things are heading in the right direction for you."

"I'm happy for you too," she said, touching his hand.

"What do you mean?" he asked, uncomfortable at her concern.

"You've never had a mother who was there for you," she said, her voice quivering. "I want to change that. It might be overdue, but I want to try." She wiped tears away with the back of her hand, smearing mascara under her eyes. Then she leaned over and put her arms around him.

Her embrace was unfamiliar to Rob, and he froze stiff, finally putting one heavy arm awkwardly around her.

"So that's all I wanted to say." She moved back, relieved, and took a napkin to wipe under her eyes. "That's enough about me, let me hear about my baby. How's school?"

"Not bad."

"What courses are you taking?"

"History, philosophy, political science and English."

"And what's your favourite?"

"Philosophy. I'm working on a term paper."

"What's it about?"

"The existence of God."

She smiled. "That's something I've spent a lot of time thinking about lately."

"Yeah, me too. We've had some hot arguments between the believers and the nonbelievers."

"Which side of the fence are you on?"

"I think science wins out over religion."

"So you don't believe in God, honey?"

"I guess not."

"Maybe what you believe in or don't believe in doesn't really matter," Mrs. Ethan said thoughtfully.

"It does to our professor."

"Of course you have to be specific in a term paper, honey, but I'm talking about real life. I speak to my Higher Power every day but I don't care if it's real or not as long as it exists for me."

"How can you say you believe in it, then?" Rob said, folding his arms.

"Let me put it this way. Do you believe there are more powerful things in the universe than yourself?"

"Probably."

"So you aren't the most powerful thing on earth, then?"

"I guess not. So what?"

"If you're not the most powerful thing, then there's something more powerful. So imagine it and make it your Higher Power. When you need an ally, it'll give you strength."

Rob sat back in his chair. "That doesn't sound like religion."

"It may not be the church's idea of a Higher Power, but at the end of the day it does the job. Take me – I need something to get me through my alcoholism each day, so I believe in a Higher Power that can make me more powerful than I was the day before. Last week I even admitted for the first time that I was an alcoholic."

Mrs. Ethan's admission of alcoholism jolted Rob. Now he was branded forever. He was from a flawed family.

"But we're getting pretty deep," she said. "We can always talk about this more later. I came over for another reason too – to ask you to join me for dinner at Bud and Jeannie's next Saturday."

"I don't know if I can," said Rob. This was all too much. First admitting she was an alcoholic, then asking him to hang out with a bunch of other alcoholics as well.

"Your father said he'd drive you."

"Umm, I have to write my term paper. Remember?"

"Look, it's just dinner. You'll like it. They live down by the river in a beautiful house."

Rob thought about meeting Bud and Jeannie in the hospital. Something had seemed different about them. "OK, OK, I'll go."

A dull pain surrounded his stomach and filled his chest cavity, making him feel heavy. This pain was new to Rob, nothing like getting hit in karate class.

Chapter 20

"What time is your dinner?" Rob's father yelled from the kitchen.

"Six-thirty," Rob hollered back from his room. He was just back from karate.

"Then we'll leave as soon as you're ready."

Dressing up for dinner was energizing. Blue jeans? Not tonight. Maybe the grey dress pants if they fit; haven't worn them for a while. Getting short but they'll do. Dusty black loafers; there, they only needed a wipe with my sweatshirt sleeve. Snug, but not too painful.

Rob grabbed the red plaid wool jacket from the coat hook at the back door and buttoned it up on his way to the car. "Frig, this seat is like ice," he said. It was nearly the middle of November and it had turned brutally cold the night before and snowed.

The defroster tried optimistically to melt away the icy layer on the windshield. Little by little, as their view opened, Rob became excited about the evening.

As they tried to back out, the rear tires whirred in the deep driveway snow. "I guess we should've shovelled, huh Dad?"

"Hey, that's your job, you little worm," his father joked. Another shot of gas made the car lurch forward and then backwards. Finally, Mr. Ethan gunned the engine and the car shot forward into the lane.

They drove into a wealthy section, where driveways snaked among trees to the affluent homes hidden behind them. All they could see as they searched for the address were lamps and addresses on posts at the street ends of the driveways. Suddenly Rob saw it. "There's 128!"

Mr. Ethan drove up the ploughed driveway and stopped in the loop in front of the house. "Pick you up at ten, Rob. Enjoy yourself."

The home was massive. Rob sounded the doorbell, producing deep chimes, and soon a familiar, wrinkled face looked up at him. "So nice to see you, Rob!" said Bud. "What's it like out there?"

"Shit … uh, shoot, it's unbelievably cold," he replied as he tripped over the oriental rug in the entrance.

Bud chuckled. "It's warm inside. Come in and sit by the fire."

A fire lit up the living room, with crackling and the occasional spark exploding into the brass screen. Two women were already in the room – his mother with crutches nearby and Jeannie.

"Hi, honey," said Mrs. Ethan as Rob leaned over to kiss her on the cheek. "You remember Jeannie."

"Pleased to meet you again, ma'am."

She gave him a firm hug. "Don't 'ma'am' me! I'm just Jeannie, for heaven's sakes. I'm glad you could join us for dinner. Your mom says such nice things about you all the time," she said, the glow from the fire lighting up her smiling face.

That was a surprise.

"What can I get you to drink?" asked Bud. "Some pop or some coffee or tea?"

"Coke would be great, thanks."

"Done."

"What do you want, Sandra?" Jeannie asked as she moved with Bud towards the kitchen."

"I'll have a cup of coffee, if it's not too much trouble." Rob was pleased; he hadn't heard her ask for anything but booze for ages.

"So, what do you think about Bud and Jeannie?" asked Mrs.

Ethan when they were alone.

"Nice. This place is something else, huh?" Rob said, looking around at the opulent furnishings.

"They're not your typical rich snob types, honey. They're special people."

Eventually Jeannie invited them into the dining room and seated them around the table. Getting through dinner with his mother sober would be a new experience, thought Rob. No sloppy stories from a drunk all night.

Then he noticed the crystal stemmed glasses on the table. Was wine going to be served with dinner? When Jeannie filled the glasses from a pitcher of icewater, he was relieved.

Next Bud and Jeannie passed around deep bowls of hearty vegetable soup that warmed Rob's stomach. Bud, who sat around a corner from Rob, slurped enthusiastically. Rob couldn't imagine he'd ever been a mean drunk.

Bud asked everyone, "So you heard the one about the guy who ordered a bowl of soup in a fancy restaurant?"

They all had, of course, but they pretended they hadn't.

"A guy goes into a restaurant and orders a bowl of soup. But when he gets it, there's a problem. 'Waiter, there's a fly in my soup.' So the waiter says, 'Quiet! If you say it too loudly, everyone will want one.'"

Rob pushed himself to smile and chuckle. His mother's face expressed giddy happiness as she let out a high-pitched laugh. She was having the time of her life.

Dinner was prime rib, cooked rare as Rob liked it. Afterwards, Rob's mother went with Jeannie into the kitchen to clear up and Bud invited Rob to go into the living room. Bud put on a jazz LP and took a pack of cigarettes out of his pocket. "Mind if I smoke?"

"Not at all," said Rob.

"Do you want one?"

"Thanks, but I'm training for a karate tournament."

"Excellent! When I was young I wanted to learn to box, but I got diverted into some other business and now I'm an old man." He gave a few hoarse coughs.

"You're not so old," said Rob politely. In truth, his wrinkles made him look about seventy.

"Well, to be honest, Rob, drinking will age you quicker than anything. That's why we're there to help your mom beat her disease."

Goosebumps spread over Rob as the topic of his mother's drinking came up.

"Jeannie's helping Sandra stay sober, you know." Bud continued. "Your mom's been dry since the accident. Longest she's been in years, I hear."

"You're right about that," Rob said, hoping this was the end of the conversation.

"She's a fine woman and she sure does love you. She's had a hellish problem with her illness, though. It's good to look at it like that – as an illness. Her addiction ran her life until now, but she's taking control back again. I'm sure her alcoholism has affected your life in a very serious way."

Rob fidgeted. There was that word again – alcoholism.

"It wasn't too bad," he muttered.

"You're being kind, Rob, but I know otherwise. Your mother wasn't always there when you needed her. But now she recognizes the hardships you went through and wants to make amends. She might not be able to fix the hurt you felt growing up, but will you give her a chance to try?"

"It'll be different, I guess." Bud's gentleness made the acceptance of his mother's struggle easier.

"She won't get better instantly. It'll take years for her to come face to face with all of her demons. But with the help of her Higher

Power, it can eventually happen. You have to try to believe that, Rob, and open yourself to her."

"I'm trying, but we've never talked about anything before," Rob complained.

"It's bloody difficult to have an intimate relationship with a drunk. But now she can be the mother you never had."

There was that pressure in his stomach coming back again. Rob sat very straight took some deep breaths. "How do I know whether or not she'll start drinking again?" he asked, holding his midsection.

"She'll always be an alcoholic and she could hit the bottle again. There are no guarantees. But if she works with Jeannie and the program it'll be her best chance to stay sober and start being a support to you, instead of the other way round."

"I'll survive."

"You need to do more than survive, Rob," said Bud forcefully. "You've been surviving your whole life. That's not fair. A boy should have a mother who can be there for him. You can't change the fact that she wasn't, but you can start thinking about yourself and making sure her mistakes don't blight your life."

"What are you talking about?" asked Rob. He wasn't supposed to be the one that needed help.

"Alcoholism is a family disease. You were affected by your mom's drinking as you were growing up, and eventually your parents separated. Now you have to ask, are you happy with who you are after having survived in that environment? If you're not, you need to get some help from friends and family."

"I haven't had it so bad," he reasoned with Bud. "Compared to my friend Julius. When his father gets drunk he beats him up and his mom, too."

"It sounds like your friend Julius is having a tough time because of the abuse in his home. His mother might be better off leaving, though that's not usually easy."

"Why not? Why can't she leave and take Julius away from his dad?"

"That's a difficult question to answer. Some abused women can't imagine living without their addicted partner. They can't imagine any other life than the one they have, so they don't believe they can make it on their own. In the end, though, they're the ones who have to make the choice; we can only be there to support them."

Jeannie called them back to the dining room for dessert. As Bud butted out his cigarette, he coughed a few more times and Rob wondered if his smoking was catching up with him. He didn't sound good.

While Rob was eating his coconut cream pie he didn't pay much attention to the adults' chatter. Instead, he thought about the discussion he'd had with Bud, wondering if the same was true for Julius – that no one could ever convince him to fix his life, that he'd have to choose to for himself. People were so alone, Rob thought, starting to imagine how each person had so much stuff going on in their heads that no one else could ever understand.

"Rob," his mother said, waving a hand in front of his face. "You missed the whole conversation we were having. I was wondering if you'd like to come with me to your cousin's wedding in Vancouver."

Her invitation was a shock, since Rob hadn't travelled since he was a child. Then he realized who would have to pay. Mrs. Ethan was out of work, so he'd have to buy his own ticket or ask his Dad, which he wasn't willing to do.

"Thanks, but I don't have the money."

Rob's mother smiled at the hosts. "Jeannie and Bud are giving us a Christmas present. They're looking after the plane tickets for us."

"I don't know if I can go," said Rob, frowning at his mother. He wasn't comfortable receiving a huge present from people who were nearly strangers.

Bud cleared his voice. "Rob, we thought it would be a chance for you and your mom to spend some quality time together."

"But it's a lot of money." He tried to think of ways they could afford the trip without Bud and Jeannie's assistance.

"Nonsense," said Jeannie. "You're a nice young man and your mother needs a date."

Rob thought, yes, he could watch over her. "OK." Bud reached over and shook his hand.

"It's settled, then, honey" said Mrs. Ethan. "I'm so excited! We'll go for Friday and Saturday night, and fly home on Sunday."

"Do I need to rent a tux?"

Bud chuckled, "Not unless you're the one getting married. But if you like I can lend you a nice navy blue blazer I've grown out of," he said, looking at his belly.

Rob turned to his mother.

"Thank you, Bud," said Mrs. Ethan. "I'm sure he'll look splendid. A navy jacket will go with the grey pants he's wearing."

"Thanks for everything," said Rob sheepishly.

"Never be embarrassed about accepting help from friends," said Bud. "It's gotten me through a few rough spots – and we've had a few together, haven't we, Jeannie?" Bud winked at his wife.

"Mostly from you. See all this grey hair?" Jeannie giggled, pointing at her head.

"You've also had your moments, my love," Bud ribbed her. He raised his water glass. "But that's all in the past. Here's to a bright, healthy and happy future for everyone."

They all raised their glasses and clinked. Rob's water glass was almost empty, but it didn't matter.

Chapter 21

Sensei asked the class to sit in a circle around him.

"Let's talk about proper breathing in *Sanchin kata,*" he said, stroking his beard. "I don't want to see you gasping for air at the tournament."

Rob knew this was his one of his problems, so he paid close attention.

"Think about drawing the breath down through the nostrils. As you inhale, your stomach should squeeze in, forcing down your diaphragm. Take a half-breath – don't fill up the lungs."

Sensei rubbed his ballooning belly. "It looks like you're fat, but that's *Sanchin* belly," he said, "Hard on the outside but soft enough on the inside to absorb a strike."

"To expel the air, explode out from the *dan tian.*" A whoosh blew from deep in Sensei's belly. "Low breathing harnesses your power, which will help you in the tournament. If the sound comes from your throat, you're breathing too high."

The class filled the room with whooshes as they tried breathing out of their bellies.

"When you attach the proper breathing technique to a strike, its called *Uechi* breathing," Sensei continued. "As you draw your arm back to strike, inhale half a breath and force down your breath, your body and your shoulders. Drop your weight below your belt to your centre of power – that way, you're loading up your power like a spring."

He began to release his arm forward. "As you begin your strike, release the energy so it will flow up and out towards your attacker. Drop it in, and at the end of the thrust, tense up all the muscles in your body to send power to the end of your strike. Then, when you expel a half-breath from your *dan tian*, you will release chi through your fingers."

The floor shook with each thrust from Sensei's arm. "When your strike is complete, let the energy recoil back into your stance. Breathe in. Think about capturing all the energy you just released and bottling it back in your body for the next strike."

"Come up here, Rob," Sensei said suddenly, motioning for Rob to stand and join him in the middle of the circle. Rob stood up and folded his arms, uncertain what to do.

"Closer. Hold your hand on my lower stomach as I strike."

Sensei pulled his fist back by his side and thrust out. At the end of the strike, Rob felt Sensei's lower stomach push out with a quick snap and heard a whooshing sound from the bottom of Sensei's stomach.

"As you develop breathing power, you'll be able to sense your entire lower body contract with the in breath and expand with the out breath."

Rob nodded as he felt this effect happening in Sensei.

"Now stand in front of me, Rob, and learn the difference between two strikes."

A familiar feeling of fear and excitement rattled through Rob's body. He was supposed to stand up there defenceless and be hit.

Sensei addressed the class. "First I'll strike Rob using regular breathing and muscle strength, no chi."

When Sensei wound up and struck, the sensation was like a wide board hitting Rob's upper chest. The pain was broad and flat, but tolerable.

"How was that Rob?" Sensei asked.

"Not bad," he smiled smugly, making the class chuckle.

"OK," said Sensei. "Now for a strike with *Sanchin* breathing."

This time Rob heard the sound of Sensei's breath expel at the end of the strike. A penetrating, hot-poker-like pain entered his chest and went out his back, numbing him. He felt the power drain from his body, his legs went weak and he stumbled back.

"Now, did you notice any difference between the first strike and second strike?"

"Ai, Sensei," Rob gasped, put his hand up to his chest and forcing a smile, "the second strike was much more powerful and painful."

The class laughed at Rob's incoherent motions.

"Now, everyone to get a partner and try. Only hit the chest muscle on the right side – if you hit the left side incorrectly you can send your partner's heart into cardiac arrest and kill him instantly. So exercise some care, please."

The class erupted in a flurry of strikes. Faces grimaced as students held out their raw chests to have the same tender spot hit repeatedly. But no one quit; everyone was motivated to learn the secret of *Sanchin* breathing.

Rob became lost in the exercise with Dave Friesen, his partner. After five or six strikes, as he moved past the pain and embraced it, his chest stopped hurting. He felt alive.

"Man, that was brutal," said Dave when they were changing. "Hope I didn't hit you too hard."

"No, I'm doing fine. How about you?"

"Sore! I'm not going in the tournament. I'll need a week to recover from this class."

Rob sensed that was just Dave's cover for his poor opinion of his own ability.

As Rob was leaving the dojo, he dropped to his knees and bowed to the floor as he always did. But this time when he came up, Sensei was standing sternly in front of him.

"Where's your registration form for the tournament? It's due tomorrow."

Rob was ashamed. "I wasn't planning to enter."

"How come?"

"Uh, my speed and power aren't really there yet."

"Go put your gi back on and we'll see about that."

For a moment Rob stood paralyzed in front of the other students, but then he moved towards the change room. He heard Sensei calling out, "Class is over, everyone, see you next time."

When he returned in his gi, Sensei was waiting for him in the middle of the floor. The rest of the room was empty.

"OK, attack me."

"What?"

"I said attack me!"

Rob advanced and threw a left punch. Sensei stepped to the side and it missed.

"Harder!"

Next Rob tried a quick left and a right front kick. Sensei blocked the punch, then grabbed Rob's right leg and swept under his left one so he hit the floor hard.

Dazed, Rob stood up and glared.

"Attack me harder," Sensei taunted, "like you want to kill me, like you're in a street fight. Come on, you can do it!"

Suddenly there was no thought, no emotion. Rob pounced forward, punching left, right, left; kicking and then thrusting a left that was blocked and a right that connected with Sensei's face.

Stopping, Rob sucked for air.

"You're ready. But watch your breathing," Sensei muttered as he checked for blood from his nose.

"Sorry."

"What? It's my fault. I didn't block it. See you Saturday at the tournament."

Chapter 22

By Friday, Rob was excited. Only one more day of classes to get through before the weekend.

At the end of philosophy class, Alana turned to Rob, "Do you have time for coffee?"

"Sure, a few minutes. I should get home and practice after that, though."

"That's right! It's your big day tomorrow, isn't it?"

"I really don't want to blow it."

"No need to be so bloody hard on yourself."

Rob shrugged and they moved in the direction of the lounge.

"I'll buy coffee for once," she said, reaching for her pink leather change purse.

"OK. Three cream and three sugar in mine, please."

"I remember – always extra sweet."

"Like you," he said with a silly grin.

"You're trying to make my day, aren't you? Go select a seat, I'll wait in line."

Rob moved to the loveseat by the window. That she usually waited for him after class was a good sign. But was she interested in more than hanging out after class? He still couldn't tell. He didn't want to blow his friendship with Alana.

"Here you go, coffee as sweet as you are," she teased.

"Thanks," he sipped it, waking himself up after a dreary class on the limits of self-knowledge.

"Where's your friend been?"

"Who?"

"You know, Mr. Longhair."

"Julius? I don't know, I haven't heard from him for a few weeks."

"Maybe he's dropped out," suggested Alana. "After all, the bloke hardly ever shows up for class."

"He's probably got some other things to do."

"Such as?"

"Art. Drugs. Women."

"And do you partake in these activities?" Alana asked coyly.

Rob sat back in his chair and smirked. "To be honest, I don't have a whole lot of experience at any of them."

"I suspected as much. You're so shy, my lad!"

"Perhaps you could help me gain some," Rob said, sipping.

"First there would have to be love. And I hardly know you."

Rob looked into his coffee cup, deflated.

"So, where is the tournament going to be held?" Alana said, running her finger around the edge of her cup.

"The Dafoe Gym. Why?"

"Just wondering. What happens at these things?"

"We perform a routine for the judges, then fight."

"Good luck!"

"Thanks, I'll need a lot more than luck not to get anything broken."

"Are you being serious?"

"Kind of."

Alana looked nervous. "Will your parents be there?"

Rob stopped cold. He wanted to make up a story, but he was sick of deception. "I didn't ask them to go because my parents aren't together."

"Oh, I'm sorry," said Alana, embarrassed. "So … what time does the fighting happen?"

"The tournament begins at ten. Why?"

"No reason. I have an appointment to go shopping tomorrow morning."

Too bad, thought Rob, as he sipped on his coffee. Why was she always raising his hopes and then dashing them?

Chapter 23

The gym was a sea of white uniforms as the teams clustered in their groups. Rob looked among them for his fellow students. Finally, he saw Billy Thomas standing alone by the far wall.

Rob walked over to Billy. "Where is everyone?" he asked, looking around.

"Not sure," Billy shrugged.

Rob sized up a team that was warming up a few yards away. They looked big and tough and were executing a sparring drill.

"You think we can take those guys?"

"No problem," said Billy wiping his nose with the back of his hand "We're *Uechi.* Whatever they give us we can give back twice as hard."

A few of their teammates came out of the locker room and joined them. Finally they saw Sensei cross the floor.

"How do you feel, gentlemen?" he asked his students.

"A-1," said Billy, grinning.

"Great," said Rob, trying to seem as confident.

The others nodded.

"Glad to hear it. Let's put on a good show."

At ten o'clock the *kata* competition started. As each contestant's name was called, his friends and family in the crowd would cheer. He would walk to the front of the room, bow and move gracefully through the form. Watching each performance carefully, Rob observed that most of the styles were unlike his own. The last student's motions were especially fast and fluid; his seemed to be the standard to beat.

Rob tensed because he was next in line. When his name was called, the cheering was sparse, although he thought he heard someone whistle. He bowed to the panel of judges and announced the name of his *kata*. "*Seisan kata.*"

As he began his form, his surroundings blurred. Each move and technique was performed quickly, without thought. Then he finished, breathing hard.

The judges raised their cards, three sevens and two eights. Applause and a few whistles came from the crowd as Rob bowed and walked back to his place.

"Pretty good, but a little fast," said Billy.

Rob agreed. The marks were respectable, but not high enough to earn a medal.

The sparring event was next. Rob stood in a line of twelve and waited to be matched for his first fight. If he lost it he would be out of the competition.

When the head referee called out two names for the first spar, one of them was Rob's. Shouts and whistles came from the crowd.

The opponent was shorter but much heavier than Rob. The referee handed him a blue belt, and Rob a red belt. They touched gloves. Rob attacked the other kid with a flurry of punches and kicks. He had decided to go on the offensive right off the mark.

When the other boy backed away from Rob's punches, he crossed the tape on the floor that marked the boundary of the ring, so the referee interrupted the match.

They went back to the middle of the ring. Rob saw a slow kick coming at him and grabbed his opponent's ankle, moving forward and pushing the leg in the air. The other boy went down hard on his butt. Rob moved on top and hit the boy lightly three times in the head, making sure not to hit his face, since that would get him a penalty.

The spar was over. Rob was surprised that the fight had been that easy. The judges in the corners of the ring pointed towards Rob's corner, and a high-pitched whistle split the air. Rob had won.

Billy gave Rob a high five. "You killed him!"

"He didn't put up much of a fight," said Rob, pleased.

Billy was up next. His opponent, Rob noticed, wore a uniform with a crest that showed he was on the provincial junior karate team. It was against the rules to show off any affiliation or accomplishment in the sparring ring, and the head referee picked up a roll of tape and covered up the boy's provincial crest.

Billy hit his opponent hard two or three times, but the other boy was faster, and scored three blows for every one Billy could land. The decision was unanimous for Billy's opponent.

Billy returned, sweating and out of breath. "He's the provincial champ," he said, justifying the loss.

As the other boy removed his headgear and gloves and went up to his team to accept congratulations, his strutting attitude irked Rob.

Now it was time for Rob's second match. The contestant chosen to oppose him was blond and well built. As soon as they started sparring Rob felt that this kid was equal to him, if not better. As he matched Rob punch for punch, Rob resigned himself to losing.

But the judges declared a tie and the referee broke it in Rob's favour. Rob heard a cheer from the stands.

"You're in the finals," said Billy, slapping Rob's hand.

"What?"

"Yeah, you're fighting for gold, man!"

Rob's spirits sank. He would have to fight that cocky provincial champ, who had not lost a bout and who had defeated Billy. Rob had watched him observing the bouts and making analytical gestures to his teammates about each fighter. He seemed to be confident he was better than anyone else.

Sensei came up to Rob for the first time since the match had begun. "You're in position to win the whole tournament. I know you have it in you."

"You think I can beat that guy?"

"Not if you keep that attitude. Then you've lost already," Sensei said in a serious tone.

"I watched him against Billy. I'm just not that fast. Would I look better if I went on the defence and countered him?"

"Forget your ego, Rob. Stop worrying about how he'll make you look. Remember, your power comes from *Sanchin.* Keep it together."

Rob stepped into the ring. His heart beat hard and he tried to shake the foggy haze that surrounded his head. "Yahoo, Rob!" shouted someone in the crowd. But Rob refused to glance up. He wanted to follow Sensei's words – to focus on staying in *Sanchin* in the fight and ignore what anyone else might think.

The first punch was a hard right hand to Rob's nose. Foul, thought Rob. The referee agreed. He stopped the fight and gave the champ a warning, and the judges deducted a point. The crowd whistled and jeered.

Rob's eyes watered and he felt fluid dripping out of his nostrils. The referee came over with a towel and called a two-minute time out. Drops of blood were staining the front of Rob's white uniform. "Keep your head back," said the referee. After a minute, when Rob took the towel away, the bleeding had stopped, but the pain hadn't.

The match was back on, but Rob was still distracted by the earlier blow. Whenever he felt something drip off his nose he looked to see if it was blood or sweat. He knew if he continued to bleed, the bout would be stopped.

Rob took three punches to the body and a kick to the gut. Then, when the champ moved in and grabbed his gi for a takedown, Rob dropped down in his stance and threw a strong right hook to the opponent's ear. The champ's head snapped back. This time Rob was issued a warning and lost a point.

As soon as the referee gave the signal to begin, the champ lunged. When Rob saw the anger in his opponent's face, he retreated and covered up, trying to block the barrage of punches and kicks. It was his same problem as always – when the fight heated up he cooled down. He could never get as angry as his opponent.

The spar ended as he'd predicted. The gold medal would go to the champ.

But just then, Rob realized that he'd also won.

He moved through the closing ceremonies in disbelief. The judges slipped the silver medal over Rob's head and he bowed back to them. Sensei shook hands with his students and stood tall beside Rob at the closing ceremony.

Then Alana came out of the stands and Rob realized that she'd been the source of the cheering and whistling for him.

"Congratulations," Alana said, putting her arms around Rob and hugging him.

"Thanks for coming," said Rob. "Sorry I didn't win."

"Silly, yes you did."

Chapter 24

Rob buttoned up his woollen plaid coat, stuck his bare hands in the pockets for warmth and set out for school. The ground was hard, the grass dead. Small puddles on the sidewalk had frozen. He breathed white vapour with each step.

When Rob got to Julius' house, he saw the dirty green Chevy in the driveway. That could have only one meaning – Julius' father was hung over and had not gone to work. Should he stop by or just keep going? Rob wanted to tell Julius about the tournament, but hated the thought of running into Mr. Stein.

Squeezing the silver medal in his pocket, Rob walked up the path to the front door and rang the doorbell. Finally Julius' father, in a bathrobe, jerked the door open.

"Oh, it's you. Corinne, would you come to the goddamn door?" He scratched his unshaven bulldog face and shuffled off.

Mrs. Stein came to the door, tying her housecoat. She put her thin fingers through her blond hair and just stood there.

"Sorry," said Rob, regretting his decision. "I wondered if Julius was going to class today."

Her hand trembled as she touched her lip. "Rob, Julius is in the hospital."

"Is it serious?" Rob asked with a feeling of déjà vu.

"Yes. We rushed him to emergency Saturday night to have his stomach pumped.

Rob was dazed, didn't know what to say. "Is he going to be OK?"

"The doctors are still assessing him."

Mr. Stein reappeared dressed for work. "You didn't tell him, did you, Corinne?" he said harshly.

"Joe, he only asked where Julius was."

"I want this kept quiet, kid. Got it?"

"Yes, sir."

"All we're saying is he got sick," Julius' father ordered, pointing at his wife and Rob. He pushed past them. "Jesus Christ, I'm really late again." A shudder sawed through Rob as the green car screeched down the street and sped away.

Julius' mom peered at the empty driveway like a scared animal checking to make sure the coast was clear. "Joe can't cope with his work; he's been drinking night and day. Last week he didn't even come home some nights. And now on top of it Julius is sick." She shook her head miserably. "But you should visit Julius; he's bad this time," she said in a trembling voice. "The doctors have to do something for him. I can't keep living through his episodes."

Rob could see she felt helpless to keep her family from falling apart. He wanted to say he was too busy to visit Julius. He didn't need another hospital drama, it was the last thing he needed. But he couldn't say no to this pleading woman.

"OK, I'll go. So he's, uh, done stuff like this before?"

Mrs. Stein nodded, looking at the ground.

"Maybe it's school," offered Rob. "It can be a lot of pressure."

"Maybe," said Mrs. Stein. "But his fights with his father aren't helping, either. They had a real bad one Friday night." She looked into Rob's eyes. "Don't tell anyone, alright?"

"I know. Which hospital is he at?"

"Western General, sixth floor. I'm so glad you're going, Rob. You're such a nice boy; maybe he'll talk to you."

As Rob turned to leave, he felt a huge weight on his shoulders. What a mistake to have made friends with Julius!

But as he walked along to school, he kept turning it over. Julius was his best friend right now. He was a really good guy; he cared about people instead of trying to impress them. And he was really sensitive, interested in getting in touch with his soul and stuff. Rob's own emotional life was probably pretty narrow compared to Julius'.

Then again, Rob was proud that he could take whatever life dished out without breaking down like Julius. Other guys his age would have crumbled if they'd had to deal with the problems he had, like his mother's drinking. Problems like that actually made life kind of interesting. Anyhow, it was what he was used to.

Chapter 25

As Rob waited at the bus stop with many other students, a blustery north wind slammed frigid air into him. The daylight was quickly disappearing. He turned his back to the wind with the others and shivered.

On the bus, Rob rubbed his finger along the moulded metal trim of the bus and thought about a conversation he'd had with Julius a few weeks ago when they'd been out for pizza.

"The workload is too heavy, man," Julius had said. "I'm late on my essay for Comparative Religions, got no energy to start it. Plus I got no time to paint. Every time I look at my empty canvases I feel even crappier."

What should he say when he saw Julius now? Should he try to cheer him up or just listen? He was used to listening to his mother's long inebriated tales of woe about her marriage or her job. It never helped, though he kept listening.

The open parking area of the Western General Hospital gave no shelter against the wind as Rob paced towards the towering building. By the time he reached the revolving doors, his face and mind were numb.

On the lobby wall was a coloured chart indicating the wards in the hospital. The sixth floor, Psychiatry, was red. Rob fought the flutter in his stomach. His finger froze on the round black elevator button.

When the elevator doors opened there was an attractive blond girl in a royal blue sweater already inside. "What floor you going to?" she asked flirtatiously.

"Five," Rob lied, not wanting to have to explain about Julius. So he'd have to walk up one flight of stairs.

"The maternity floor," she cooed. "Me too! My sister had a baby. How about you?"

"Uh, my mom," he stuttered.

"Cool. Do you have a little brother or sister?"

His mind was blank. "I'm not sure."

"Why not?" she asked, grinning.

"Uh, she just had it."

"Did you want a brother or sister?"

"I guess a brother."

"Are you sure you're not a new father?" She giggled.

"I'm sure," Rob muttered.

The elevator doors opened on the fifth floor and they walked out together. "Have fun babysitting," she said as she walked off down a pink hallway decorated with pictures of children.

When she had turned the corner, he looked for the stairwell.

The sixth floor was totally different. It was pale green and smelled like disinfectant, and most of the doors were closed. A white-haired man walked into Rob, babbled something about the devil and kept going.

A heavy-set nurse with short red hair looked up from her paperwork as he approached.

"I'd like to see Julius Stein. Could you tell me what room he's in?"

"Twenty-two," she said, barely looking up.

As Rob walked towards Julius' room, a woman about his mother's age shuffled along beside him in a housecoat. Her uncombed hair was dyed blond and her pale face was empty.

The door was half open, so Rob knocked softly and then ventured in. He could barely see – the only light in the room was the last glimmer from the setting sun, dimmed by the metal security screen on the window.

All Rob could see in the first bed was a lump under a blanket. Julius lay in the second bed on his side, eyes open. He looked pale and thin, his long hair tangled and messy. He turned his head and looked blankly in Rob's direction.

"How ya doing, man?" said Rob.

"Crappy."

What could he say to that? "Your mom said it would be OK if I dropped in."

"Fine." Julius still hadn't looked directly at Rob.

"When are you going to get your butt out of here and come back to school?" Rob said, trying to be upbeat.

"I ain't coming back."

"What's the matter, man?"

"Nothing's the matter. I just want to kill myself."

This visit was clearly a mistake, thought Rob. But he'd have felt even worse if he hadn't tried to connect with Julius.

"You shouldn't think about that, man. People care about you."

"But I don't care about anything" said Julius, dropping his head down on the pillow.

An easel holding a canvas and a paint box stood against the wall. It looked like Julius had started to prep the canvas.

"What's your painting going to be?" asked Rob, trying to find a subject Julius would respond to.

"I can't paint, my work is lousy."

Rob recalled Julius' watercolours of rolling landscapes, rustic barns and old country houses. "Your work is not, Julius. It's great.

You only need to get on your feet."

"I can't do anything any more."

"Jeezus, Julius," Rob pleaded, "you're a great artist. Why are you being so hard on yourself?"

Julius stared at Rob blankly.

"Is your father hassling you?" probed Rob, thinking about what Mrs. Stein had said.

"I can't deal with him any more, he's a psycho."

Rob sat back in his chair. Finally Julius had some emotion in his voice.

"He started at me for not making it to school. I just didn't feel like going. I wanted to stay home and paint. So he lost it."

"What did he do?"

"He put his fist through my paintings. Every one."

"Geez." That was way worse than anything Rob's mother had ever done.

"I spent years working on them and he smashed it all," said Julius, looking like a bewildered child. "When I tried to grab a picture back from him he slugged me."

That's insane, thought Rob. Julius dropped his head down on the pillow.

"It's all right, man," said Rob, putting his hand on Julius' side and glancing out the window.

After a few minutes, he tried to start up another conversation. "I've been sitting with Alana in class a lot."

"I just want to die," was all Julius could say. He rubbed his eyes with his fists.

"Hey, you gotta try to pull yourself out of this," said Rob.

"I can't."

"Have you tried, man?"

"I don't want to do anything."

“If you don’t try you won’t get better and get back to school.”

“I’m quitting.”

Rob was stunned. “Geez, Julius, you only missed a few weeks. You can catch up easy, you’re smarter than anyone else.”

“I can’t deal with it. It’s too much.”

Rob remembered how his own stomach had been in knots during the first few weeks of school about his ability to do the work.

“They’re going to give me shock treatments,” Julius mumbled.

“What’s that?”

“They jolt you with electricity and it’s supposed to make you happy, but I don’t know.” Julius looked up to Rob for some direction.

The image of Julius being strapped in a death-row type of electric chair flashed across Rob’s mind. “Well, if the doctors think it’ll help, I guess, eh?”

A tiny Filipino nurse came in the room. “Julius, dear, time for your meds,” she said, her face warm and giving.

She held out a small clear cup with pills, and Julius sat up and wiped his eyes with his pyjama sleeve. He tipped the pills into his mouth and washed them down. After a few minutes, Rob watched Julius’ eyelids grow heavy and his eyes close. He looks peaceful, Rob thought as he left.

Chapter 26

All he could see from his bed was a solid dark grey sky. Of the roaring winds of the approaching storm, Julius could hear nothing. Slowly pushing himself up, he looked for the cup of water next to his bed to wet his throat in the dry hospital air. But it was gone. He remembered, no food allowed.

A male nurse pushed him down the hall in a wheelchair and they entered a small operating room. He lay down on the bed and waited for the procedure to begin.

A doctor with white hair and a rosy complexion pushed a long needle into his arm.

"Jeezus, that hurts," he said, squirming.

The nurse held his arm steady and taped the needle in place so clear fluid from the IV above steadily entered his arm. "You won't feel anything in a moment, son."

Within a minute his eyes closed.

The nurse left the room and another doctor in thick black glasses came in and checked Julius' pulse on the monitor. "Vital signs normal," he wrote on the medical chart.

A female nurse taped electrodes to each side of his head and to the middle of his forehead. "Tighten up the straps on his legs and chest," ordered the doctor. The nurse plugged the ends of the electrodes into a black box the size of a briefcase.

"Let's go to level six today. I think he can take it," said the doctor.

The nurse pushed a red button on the black box. First Julius' body was still. But then his fingers wiggled and his toes twitched, and in several seconds his fists clenched and his chest heaved in the air.

"We'll do two more at six and go to level seven on the last one."

A fierce snowstorm had engulfed the city, grinding it to a halt until the orange plows could clear the large drifts off the streets. Rob spent the afternoon in the driveway heaving shovels of snow, trying to keep up with the accumulation.

By the time the driveway was partly clear his leather gloves were soaked. He stood back and watched the steam from his breath cloud around his mouth.

A rumbling at the end of the lane preceded the passing of the snowplow. In mere seconds, a snowplow deposited a large dirty-white ridge across the end of the driveway. Great, thought Rob. But he attacked the new pile, which had large chunks of ice mixed with the powdery snow.

After he finished, Rob joined his father in the kitchen for a cup of coffee.

"Sorry I didn't help. I didn't realize it was so heavy."

"It's OK, I need the exercise."

"How was your visit to the hospital?"

"Weird. Julius was pretty bad."

"You mean, sick from the pills he took?"

"No, down. He has no confidence. He said he's going to have shock therapy today."

"Wow, my aunt had that years ago; something to do with brain seizures. I didn't even know they still did it."

"I hope it doesn't fry his brain."

"It's supposed to be safe. Your memory goes for a while, though."

“How can Julius even decide whether he should have it or not, if he’s so depressed?” Rob worried.

“I suppose his parents gave consent.”

“Great. His old man doesn’t even know what planet he is on.”

“You probably should go see him again. I can drop you at the hospital this afternoon on the way to work.”

Rob grimaced. “You think?”

Chapter 27

Rob's anxiety mounted as he rode the elevator to the sixth floor. In the hallway he saw the old man walking back and forth, muttering.

Rob walked right past the nurse's station to room twenty-two and opened the door. The room was empty. So he went around the corner in the patients' lounge. Julius was not among the patients watching the soap opera.

He walked back to the nurses' station, where the large red-headed nurse was writing up charts. "Excuse me, but can you tell me where Julius Stein is?"

The nurse raised her head. "Oh, Julius should be in his room."

"He's not. And I already looked in the patient lounge."

"Try there again, and if you can't find him, then come back and see me." She went back to her charts.

Rob's heart leapt as a piercing scream came from down the hall.

"It's nothing," said the nurse automatically. "Don't worry about it."

Heading towards the lounge, Rob stepped into Julius' room; his bed was still empty. But this time an old man with sparse white hair was sitting up in the bed next to Julius'.

The man motioned for Rob to come near. "Grapes. Have you got grapes?" he sputtered.

"No, sorry."

"California grapes. I'm from California. There's earthquakes every day there, son, did you know that? They rattle your brain."

"Uh, excuse me," said Rob. "Have you seen Julius? The kid in the next bed?"

"Him? They took him away weeks ago. There's nobody there, now."

Rob wondered if he had come into the wrong room. But no, there was Julius' canvas by the window.

"Excuse me," Rob tried again. "About the kid in the next bed. Did they move him to another room?"

"He died. They took his eyes, you know. But they're not getting mine," the old man said fiercely. "Have you got grapes?"

Rob backed out the room and tried the lounge again. This time, he saw Julius in the far corner by the window.

"Hey, Julius," Rob called as he walked towards his friend, relieved.

Julius looked in Rob's direction but didn't say anything.

"I though I'd drop in again to visit."

"Huh?"

Rob worried about Julius' memory.

"You know me, eh?"

"Yah."

"Did you have the treatment?

Julius didn't answer and looked puzzled, as if he was searching for words that weren't there. "Today."

He seemed even worse than Rob had expected. "Sharpstein asked about you. He wants to know if you'll be back at school after Christmas."

"Who?" Julius touched his temple.

"Our philosophy professor, remember?"

"Yeah."

"He wants to know if you'll be back at school."

"Don't think so."

"Oh yeah, and I went out with Alana last week. She sits next to me every class now."

Julius looked lost, he didn't answer.

Rob put his hand on Julius' arm. "Things are kind of fuzzy, hey?"

"Yeah, my memory is bad now."

"Maybe it'd be better if I dropped in and saw you next week, huh? That is, if you aren't home."

"Good, that's cool," said Julius in a monotone.

Suddenly he brightened up. "Do you want to see my painting?"

"Sure, let's go," said Rob, regaining hope.

Julius flicked on the fluorescent light in his room. The old man was fast asleep.

Rob tried to make out the scene in the picture on the easel. It was the view from Julius' window, except the wintry trees were painted with bright dancing red and orange leaves. Instead of a parking lot in front of the hospital there was a lush grassy area where two children were chasing each other. The sky wasn't finished and the driveway needed to be put in, but the trees were beautiful.

"This is your greatest painting, Julius. You haven't forgotten how to paint, eh?" Dumb comment, thought Rob.

"I just move my hands. I don't have to think about it."

"It's amazing."

"You can have it when it's done."

"Really?"

"Yeah. I'll bring it home for you."

"It's a deal, man," said Rob, slapping Julius' hand.

"Deal," Julius replied vaguely and lay down to rest.

On the bus ride home there were two playful children sitting in front of Rob. They laughed and squealed as they hid their faces behind the seats, playing peek-a-boo while their mother read a magazine. They reminded him of the children in Julius' painting. Then one of the little boys started swinging on a pole. He wore a shirt with a red cartoon dragon on it.

As Rob smiled at the boy's shirt, his mind turned to the image of the dragon. That was the answer, a dragon, what could be better than that? Yes, that would work.

Chapter 28

When Rob stopped in to visit Julius at home the following weekend, his friend greeted him with a paint-brush in hand.

"How's it going, man?" said Julius, offering Rob his left hand because his right was smeared with paint. He led Rob into the downstairs bedroom. It was tidy for a change, with all the paint tubes lined up in perfect rows on the table by the easel.

"Like it?" asked Julius, pointing at a painting of fall foliage with dancing colours. It was the painting from the hospital, now closer to completion.

"It's wicked, I'll put it in our living room," Rob said, relaxing into the beanbag chair.

Julius looked puzzled. "Did I tell you I'd give you this one?"

"Don't worry, it's OK."

"No, it's yours. Something to remember me by."

"What do you mean?" asked Rob, worried.

Julius flipped his hair back and chuckled, enjoying Rob's panic. "Heading west in January."

"Really?"

"School in Vancouver, man. My counsellor and I kicked it around. I couldn't get into the art school this time of year, but the community college will take a flunky like me into graphic arts and then I can apply for art school for the fall."

"Cool!"

"Time to get away from my old man. I drive him crazy, he drives me crazy."

"I hear ya," said Rob, recalling that things had become a lot easier for him after his mother left. Living with a drunk wasn't pleasant.

"So, you want to go outside and have a toke?" said Julius. "I got some good stuff."

Rob was surprised and concerned that Julius was doing drugs already. "Sorry, I gotta head out, man. I'm going with Alana for pizza, then we're finally going to catch *Jaws*."

"Lucky guy. Score with her yet?" leered Julius.

Rob laughed. "Won't be easy. She's pretty innocent."

"Oh no! That makes two of you. You're gonna need some of my tips if you're ever gonna get her going."

"Like?"

"Stick your tongue in her ear. Works every time."

"Sure, I'll try walking up and doing that right in the middle of exams."

"Right on," said Julius, as he walked to his dresser. "How about one of these for the road, bro? Give you confidence with Alana." He pried off the cap from a vial of red-and-yellow pills.

"What's that?" said Rob, alarmed.

"Make you feel good, speeds you up. You know." He swallowed two capsules and chased them down with a swig from his Coke.

Rob sagged in the chair and stared. "Do you think that's cool right now, doing that stuff?"

"You sound like my old man. Telling me what to do."

"I'm not telling you what to do. I'm just worried what that shit is going to do to you."

"All you do is worry, worry, worry, man. It's nice to fly once in a while. You need to try it sometime."

Julius picked up a paintbrush and started painting bright blue streaks in the sky on the canvass, and Rob knew it was time to leave.

"See you later man," Rob said, hurrying up the stairs.

"Cool."

A blond girl is shedding her jeans and T-shirt as she runs down the slope of the sand dune towards the water. "C'mon!" she's yelling at her boyfriend, who's staying behind on the beach. "Whoops!" she's yelling as the seawater sweeps over her. There's a swell in the water a dozen feet away, and then it's right in front of her.

"Oh, my God!" Alana whispered loudly, digging her sharp fingernails into Rob's hand.

"It's just a movie," Rob whispered back.

"That doesn't mean it's not scary!

The blond girl is calling out "Tommy? Don't dunk me!" But he's still on the beach, trying to get his pants off. She's starting to swim back to shore when suddenly her expression freezes. The bulge of water is racing towards her. It's bumping her, and her hips are rising above the water.

Alana dropped her death grip on Rob's fingers and covered her face. "Lord, I'm not sure I can sit through this."

"I'll tell you when the gory part is over."

"Please, yes."

The blond girl is opening her mouth to scream, but the thing under the water is slamming her over and over and then swinging her around in the water. She's going under and the water is choking the scream. She's being pulled under; only her hair is swirling on the surface. Then it's sucked below with a final jerk, the swirls quiet, and she's gone.

For the next hour and a half, Alana peeked through her fingers at the screen, screamed twice and grabbed Rob repeatedly. Rob tried over and over to calm her.

The crowd pushed out of the theatre onto the street, buzzing with excitement.

"Thank God it's over," said Alana, holding Rob's arm tightly. "I've never seen anything so scary."

Rob chuckled, "I'd see it again in a minute, but only with you."

She gave him a light punch and smiled. "Would you care to come over?" she asked, looking in her purse for her car keys. "My parents are out for the evening."

"Sure!"

Alana started the car. "Didn't you go see Mr. Longhair before the show?" she asked, keeping her eyes on the road.

"Yup," said Rob, looking out at the downtown lights.

"So how is he?"

"He's coming around – back to painting and stuff. He's even going to go to art school. Leaving after New Year's to go to Vancouver."

"Good riddance. I never knew what you saw in him."

"He's a free spirit, you know? Tries to be a friend in his weird way. Offered me a few pills before the movie to loosen up."

Darn, Rob thought. Should have kept that to himself.

"See, I told you he's a crackpot. Those drugs will do him in."

"He'll survive. He's lived on the edge forever."

"Time will tell."

"Should I see what's on the radio?"

"John Cleese is so hilarious," said Alana, wiping tears of laughter from her eyes as they watched *Fawlty Towers* on the sofa in the rec room.

"I love this episode," said Rob, sunk into the cushions on the flowered couch.

He reached over to dry her cheek with his shirt sleeve and was startled when Alana slid around to meet his lips. They were actually kissing.

After a minute he touched her chest. She breathed heavily as his fingers found a button on her blouse and he one-handedly unbuttoned it. Wow, he thought.

He tried resting his hand on her thigh, and she didn't seem to mind. He edged the hand up a few inches at a time, pushing her skirt with it.

"Red light," she said, taking his hand and pushing it down softly.

"Sorry."

"Don't be. I started it," she said, sitting up and sweeping her hand through her hair.

Rob picked up the remote control. "So what else is on TV?"

Chapter 29

"You are even more beautiful than Rob described," Jeannie said, kissing Alana on the cheek.

"It's wonderful to meet you," Alana said. "Happy New Year."

"So what did you kids do for New Year's Eve?" asked Jeannie as a man in a tuxedo led them to their table.

"We went to a social at school. It was fun, wasn't it?" Rob said, turning to Alana.

"Yes, lots. They turned the room into a disco," said Alana.

They paused, taking in the restaurant. "This is a really nice place," said Rob, looking around at the mahogany trim and red velvet walls.

"Wait till you taste the steaks," said Bud. "They're famous."

"I can't wait," Rob said enthusiastically. "Where's my mom?"

"She's not here yet," said Jeannie, smiling.

Rob's excitement evaporated. Surely she wouldn't be late for dinner when she was going to be meeting Alana for the first time. "Maybe I'll give her a call. Is there a pay phone?"

"We'll ask the waitress to bring a phone to the table," said Jeannie. "Excuse me, waiter?"

They watched her dial and wait for a moment.

"No answer," Jeannie said.

"Super," Rob said glumly.

"So Rob," said Bud, "how did you do in that karate tournament?"

"Only second."

"Rob, coming in second means you won," Alana scolded, slapping his hand. "You got a medal and they don't give those out to everyone."

"Absolutely right," said Bud. "I'd go further and say that having the guts to compete is the most important victory. I don't think I could get into a ring with a guy who intended to beat me up. I admire that in you, Rob."

"Thanks," said Rob, blushing. "I don't always feel that gutsy when I'm in there. Sometimes I want to run right out of the ring and out the door."

"Ah, so that's the truth of it? Everybody's afraid on the inside? I'm glad to hear it."

"Why don't we order salads?" suggested Jeannie. "I'm sure Sandra will be along in a moment."

The salads arrived, but not Mrs. Ethan. Rob picked at the lettuce in his bowl and rolled the cherry tomato around on his fork. It was stupid of him to have invited Alana for dinner, he thought. He should have known his mother wasn't reliable. What would Alana think of him now? Her family was so perfect.

When the entrees were served Mrs. Ethan still hadn't arrived. Rob had no appetite and barely picked at his steak, even though it was grilled rare the way he liked it.

Bud raised another topic. "So tell us about school. What was your favourite class?"

"Philosophy, especially ethics," said Alana. "The line that divides right from wrong."

"Ah, ethics," said Bud, polishing off his last spare rib and leaning back in his chair. "An interesting topic. For instance, what do you do if someone asks you to lie for him? I was once in that position, when a young man I was sponsoring told me he had robbed a corner store, totally drunk, just to get cash for his rent and a few cases of booze. I had already read about the robbery in the paper."

"What did you do?" asked Alana, wide-eyed.

"I decided I'd be a better friend if I put him in the position where he had to face his crime and his life. He might not like me very much in the short term, but he'd have a better chance of liking himself in the long term. So I told him if he didn't turn himself in, I would call the police. In the end, he called them himself."

"I completely understand," said Alana.

Rob, who was thinking about how his mother always ruined everything, barely heard the conversation.

After Alana and Jeannie had excused themselves to go to the restroom, Bud broke the silence. "Don't look so glum, Rob."

"I guess the trip to Vancouver is dead. She's back to her old ways."

"Wait and see, it may only be a small bump in her road to recovery."

"Maybe she'll crash again then," Rob said sarcastically.

"Listen, Rob. People have slips now and again. This time of year is especially difficult. I am not condoning her behaviour, but there's not much we can do. We have to let her go her own way."

"So you're not going to give her hell?"

"Nope."

"Why? She deserves it."

Bud lit a cigarette and blew smoke in the air. "A lecture never cured a drunk, Rob. It's best if we let it go and focus on our own sanity. We can't keep trying to figure out how to change an alcoholic's behaviour or they learn to resent us. They have to do it on their own with our support when they call on it."

"I was hoping that when we went to Vancouver I'd get to see Julius."

"You might, Rob. She could bounce back."

"I doubt it. What was that you said before? Once a drunk always a drunk."

"That wasn't how I meant it," Bud defended. "We have to be grateful for the times when she is well and be there for her when she hits her low spots. One thing you'll learn, Rob, is you can't beat yourself up because bad things happen. The world is a difficult place and our only obligation is to do our best."

Alana and Jeannie returned to the table and to Rob's relief, Bud let the discussion about Rob's mother drop. Everyone said goodbyes and exchanged hugs in the restaurant to avoid standing outside in the –30° cold.

"Did you still want to me to drop you at Julius' house?" Alana asked as they shivered in the car.

"He leaves tomorrow morning, so I really should say goodbye," said Rob, not looking forward to it.

"I hoped you'd come to my place. My parents are out tonight."

Rob thought of the soft sofa in Alana's basement. It would sure be a nice ending to a crappy evening. "Would you wait for me outside, then? I won't be long."

Julius' basement bedroom had returned to its usual disarray, with Coke bottles and paint tubes scattered all over the furniture and floor.

"Hey man, thanks for dropping by. If you come to Vancouver next month, we'll have some good times," said Julius, sending Rob a wild glance.

"Now I don't know if it'll even happen. My stupid mother is screwed up again."

"So piss on her! Come alone."

"That's a neat idea … I do have a ticket, and I could go to the wedding by myself. I wonder if my father'd go for it."

"Work on it and I'll line up the babes," Julius grinned.

Rob thought of Alana waiting for him in the car. "I'm not sure about that part," he smiled.

"Good, more babes for me, then. But be prepared to party it up with us," Julius said enthusiastically. He opened the drawer of his dresser and took out his red-and-yellow pills again, gulping more than one.

He's heading for trouble, thought Rob. He can't see it because he's so messed up.

Julius saw Rob's expression. "Don't be so uptight. It's not heavy shit."

"I just think you gotta try to take care of yourself. Stay positive about the move and stuff."

"That won't be hard. It'll be heaven not having my father shoving a stick up my butt all the time. I'm never coming back here, except in a box some day." He moved forward and hugged Rob. "See you in Vancouver."

"Cool," said Rob. It was hard to return the embrace.

When he got back to the car, he put on the radio and gave Alana a big smile in the dark. What a relief, he thought, to be looking into the face of someone who had her act so together.

Chapter 30

Rob peered out his iced-over bedroom window. It was his flying day and was relieved to see clear sky. The blizzard forecast for the February weekend hadn't arrived yet.

According to his father Mrs. Ethan still planned to make the trip. Rob hadn't spoken to her since New Year's, but Bud and Jeannie had told Rob that she still hadn't sobered up.

He neatly folded the sports jacket Bud had given him into his small blue suitcase. On top, he placed the white shirt and silk tie he had purchased downtown, for half of the hundred-dollar bill his father had given him. The other half he'd spent on a silver tray for his cousin.

"Forgetting something?" Rob's dad asked, standing in the bedroom doorway.

"What?"

"This," said Mr. Ethan holding up the elegantly wrapped gift box. "And this, too," he said, handing Rob a small wad of money. "For hotel and food."

Rob took the money and put it into his pocket. He felt guilty taking the money. Since his mom's accident, she hadn't been working and his dad had to support her.

When he opened the back door cold air bit into his face. His dad unplugged the electric cord to the block heater and turned the ignition. The engine barely turned over. This damn car better not stall today, Rob thought. But Mr. Ethan gave the engine another rev and the car chugged forward down the street. Rob peered back at the house as they drove away. The upcoming trip seemed like a dream.

"Uncle Tom will be meeting you at the gate," said Mr. Ethan. "Do you have his phone number in case you miss him?"

"Yes, Dad."

"You'll call me when you get to the hotel?"

"Yes," said Rob, exercising patience.

"You meeting up with Julius tonight?"

"Yup."

"Be good."

Joining the check-in line at the airport, Rob and his dad encountered a buzz of activity – people hugging, kids yelling, porters stacking luggage. A red-faced man argued with a ticket agent over a stack of taped-up boxes he was trying to ship with him. A small child grabbed Rob's pant leg until his parents recaptured their toddler.

For several minutes the line barely moved, and Rob began checking the clock hanging from the ceiling. Suddenly a familiar figure was walking in his direction and Mrs. Ethan called out, "I made it, honey." Everyone turned to look.

"I don't believe it," said Rob's dad. Mrs. Ethan seemed sober and looked better than she had for ages. Her hair was styled and her makeup was carefully applied. She wore a new black cloth coat with a spotted fur collar. Only her old salt-stained leather boots looked out of place.

She joined the end of the line. "Come back here, honey, so we get seats together," she called. As Rob carried his suitcase back in the line, Mr. Ethan walked over to the window.

"Sorry, Rob," Mrs. Ethan said, looking sincerely into Rob's eyes. "I guess I have to make a commitment to stop living only for myself, huh?"

Rob nodded. So she was sober, good. But was this just another brief interlude in her sad life?

Mr. Ethan came over and said goodbye. He looks glum, thought Rob, as they shook hands.

As they boarded the airplane, the smell of food hit Rob's nostrils and he realized he was starving. He grabbed a sports magazine out of the seat pocket to keep his mind busy while they took off.

"I assume Uncle Tom is picking us up at the airport. You think I've had a colourful life? That guy was a handful when he was young. But he's straightened his life out – made lots of money too."

Rob kept his nose in his magazine.

When the coffee and bar trolley rolled down the aisle, a man in the row ahead ordered a vodka and orange juice even though it was only eleven in the morning. Rob got worried. The last thing he wanted was his mom slurping back free booze on the three-hour flight.

"Orange juice, please," Rob told the stewardess and froze as his mother was asked what she wanted.

"Coffee, black," Mrs. Ethan said matter-of-factly and lit a cigarette.

Meanwhile, the man ahead of them ordered his second vodka and orange juice. Every time he got up to go to the bathroom, he made the stewardess roll the bar cart to the back of the plane to let him by.

Rob and his mother barely talked during the flight. When the meals came, Rob wolfed his down silently. What could he say to her, he thought, after the rollercoaster ride she'd taken him on?

Finally, as they neared touchdown, Mrs. Ethan turned to him. "Rob, can you put that magazine down for a second? I want us to have a talk before all the relatives are around."

"OK," he said sulkily.

"You probably didn't think I was going to make this trip, huh?"

"Had my doubts."

"So did I. Then, a few days before the trip, I asked my Higher Power to help me get sane and sober. So far it's holding up. I hope you're not disappointed?"

"No." That wasn't entirely truthful, since now he had to keep an eye on her.

She looked down at her red fingernails. "I know I've messed up in the last few months and I'm sorry. But this time I'm going to stick to my program. I mean it."

Rob was silent. He had no words to respond to his mother's promise, only nagging memories of disappointments.

"We'll have a great weekend together," Mrs. Ethan pleaded as they approached touchdown.

Rob thought, we'll see.

Rob spotted Uncle Tom instantly, remembering him from when he had visited Winnipeg five years ago. He was well dressed and had a thin moustache and the same blue eyes as Mrs. Ethan.

She was enjoying the shock on Uncle Tom's face. "I thought only Rob was coming," he said, laughing and hugging her.

"Surprise!"

"Honey, nothing you do surprises me any more." Uncle Tom extended his hand to Rob. "Who's this grown-up young man? You look a lot like your mother now."

"People always say that."

"You look good too, Sandra."

"You too, Tom. Put on a few pounds, though."

Uncle Tom smiled and patted his stomach.

The sun was shining and when they walked through the sliding doors with their bags, Rob was struck by the majestic snow-capped mountains. The breeze smelled of salt air.

As they drove, Rob was thrilled to see the city opening up like a map. When they pulled up at the hotel and the bellman in his maroon uniform wheeled their bags over the marble floor, he felt very special. He looked around at the massive chandeliers and carved woodwork in the lobby and thought, this is really living.

"I hope I can bring you right over to our house for dinner. Carol is whipping up something special."

Mrs. Ethan looked at Rob. "I'll be there, but Rob is meeting up with a friend from home, aren't you?"

"Uh, yeah. Sorry."

"No problem at all. Is your friend studying here?" asked Uncle Tom.

"Yeah, graphic arts at a community college. He's an excellent painter."

"Hey, send him over. I need my house done!"

Rob laughed, "That would be interesting."

"See you at the wedding tomorrow. Sandra, I'll wait for you in the lobby."

Their room was as fancy as the lobby. It had two beds with fluffy, silky comforters and a big TV in a cabinet.

"When are you going to call Julius?" Mrs. Ethan asked as she reapplied her lipstick.

"He probably isn't home from school yet."

"But he's picking you up?"

"Supposedly. He's got an old beater."

"Does he know where we're staying?"

"Yes, mother!"

"OK, dear. Make sure not to get into any trouble and be back by midnight." She kissed him on the cheek and walked out the door.

Rob opened the heavy drapes and stared out at the tall downtown skyline framed by massive mountains. This place was so different from home. Julius wasn't supposed to call till after six, so he could explore this strange world!

After consulting a map from the concierge's desk, he walked towards Gastown, the old warehouse district. With the onset of dusk, the lights of the tall buildings glittered in the background. Young panhandlers held out cups for money and somewhere a saxophone tooted in the darkening streets. Funky music shops and cafes with neat names lined the street.

Further on, Rob noticed dealers hawking grass and heroin and prostitutes lounging on the street corner. Time to turn back.

It was just before six when he returned to the hotel. Rob waited fifteen minutes for the phone to ring and then called his friend.

Julius' phone rang three times and someone answered.

"Julius?"

"Nope," a male voice replied.

"Is Julius there?"

"Nope."

"It's his friend Rob from out of town. He and I were going to get together tonight, but he hasn't turned up."

"Haven't seen him for days."

"Do you know where he is?"

"Nope. All I know is his stuff is gone and the bugger took my eight-tracks."

"Who are you?"

"Randy, the roommate."

"Has he been around school?"

"Not that I've seen. Partying downtown, mostly."

Rob's stomach tightened. "That's not new. Julius always did stuff."

"I'm talking heavy shit."

"Like?"

"Smack. He's seriously fucked up."

"Please, if he comes in, tell him to call me right away. 634-3434, room 412."

"I'll tell him a lot more than that when I see him. I'm pissed, man."

"Are you sure it was him? That doesn't sound like Julius."

"Junkies are thieves, man."

"Listen, see if you can get him to call me. I'm here all weekend."

"Sure, whatever."

Rob hung up and turned the TV on, cranking up the volume. He watched with a blank stare for a few hours and went to bed long before midnight.

Chapter 31

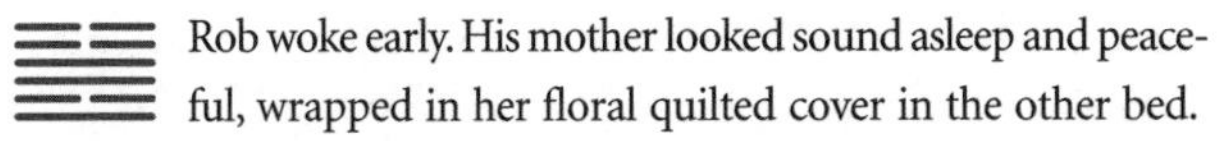

Rob woke early. His mother looked sound asleep and peaceful, wrapped in her floral quilted cover in the other bed.

He was hungry – he hadn't eaten supper the night before – so he dressed quietly and rode down to the lobby. The doorman leaned against the gold-plated front doors and the restaurant wasn't open yet. So he walked downstairs to the spa, which had huge potted trees and glass skylights, and watched an old guy swim laps for a while in the long, narrow pool.

At eight the restaurant opened. A hostess offered him the buffet, but Rob looked at the price and ordered bacon and eggs instead.

When he came back to the hotel room, his mother was dressed and brushing her hair. The room was already full of cigarette smoke.

"You were home early last night," said Mrs. Ethan. "So how's Julius?"

"I didn't see him."

"Why not?"

"Don't know. His roommate hasn't seen him for days."

"Well, honey, obviously he isn't the kind of friend you can count on."

A remark about her own reliability leapt to his mind, but he kept quiet.

The wedding ceremony was boring. Rob couldn't add to the

beaming smiles. The couple expected joy, but they were more likely to get pain. His parents' and Julius' parents' marriages were hell, not bliss.

The kissing and hugging after the wedding service was equally uninviting. Rob lurked in a side aisle away from the intimacy and commotion. His mother stood next to Uncle Tom and kissed every person who happened by, her makeup running from tears.

Rob escaped outside, but the whole congregation followed him out to the parking lot to watch the bride and groom crawl into a white limo decorated with pink flowers.

"Wave, Rob," his mother urged, but as the bridal car honked its way out of the parking lot, Rob kept his arm down.

The whole joyful occasion started all over at the reception in a fancy ballroom in their hotel. In the receiving line everyone shook hands with the men and kissed the women. When Rob came to the bride, she thanked him for coming and showed him her cheek; he shook her hand and moved on.

Duty done, he looked for his table. There was his mother at the bar, ordering a drink! He felt his skin shrivel into goose bumps. She'll be hammered before long and will become the life of the wedding party and embarrass me to death, he thought. Dejected, he sat down at his table and waited for the inevitable.

"Why don't you go up and get something to drink?"

Rob wouldn't look at her, just ripped a blue paper napkin in half.

"What's wrong with you?"

"Nothing."

"Tell you what – you take my drink and I'll go get another one."

He sipped and sniffed – it was just Coke. Ashamed, he offered, "Do you want me to go get you another one?"

"No, dear, you sit and relax. I said I'd get it."

Some of the groom's relatives had been placed at the table.

The groom's cousin Wendy was his age and had long blond curly hair with a white flower in it. She was wearing a pink formal with a neckline that didn't hide much. Rob sat up straight as she plunked down next to him.

"Hi! It's nice to have someone else my age at the table," she said, sipping her champagne.

"Yeah … are you in university?"

"Second year, science, majoring in biology. You?"

"First year arts, majoring in philosophy and English."

"You'll have to write me a poem," she said flirtatiously.

"About what?"

"You decide."

When the salad with perfectly cut radishes and tomatoes was served, Wendy said to Rob in a low voice, "Isn't this all so silly?"

"Yes. What a waste of money," said Rob honestly.

"I have no intention of getting married," said Wendy. "Well, unless I decide to have a family. But that seems unlikely – I'd rather have a career and travel."

"I know what you mean. There are a lot of places I'd like to see," said Rob.

"Like where?

"Japan, China. I'd like to tour those places, maybe see some martial arts stuff."

"Neat!"

Over dessert she asked, "So do you have a girlfriend?"

Rob assessed whether Alana fit the description. They weren't going steady.

"Not really."

"I just broke up with my boyfriend. All he wanted to do was have sex and then go out and drink beer."

Rob just nodded, not knowing how to respond.

The bride and groom finished their ceremonial waltz, and Wendy dragged Rob onto the dance floor for the disco tunes. She really let go in a sensuous style, unlike Alana, who danced with reserve.

A slow song began and Wendy grabbed Rob. "Let's do this one too," she said. He couldn't refuse. She pressed against him and swayed back and forth with his motion.

At the end of the song, Wendy surprised Rob by kissing him. He was slightly embarrassed about making a scene in the middle of the dance floor. This girl didn't seem to have any inhibitions.

"Did you mind?" she asked shamelessly.

"Not at all."

"That's good. Let's go for a walk."

They walked out to the lobby and sat down in a long sofa, and Wendy immediately took his hand and put his arm around her shoulder. Rob couldn't believe how easy it was to make out with this girl, compared to Alana.

"Are you staying in the hotel?" asked Wendy.

"Yeah," said Rob.

"Can I see your room?"

Rob's heart pounded as they walked towards the elevators. She kissed him on the way up and continued to kiss him as he unlocked the room door. Then she made a beeline to the one lighted lamp and turned it off.

Half an hour later, Rob began to worry about his mother coming in. "This is nice, but we really shouldn't stay in here too long," he moaned.

"Damn," she said, "I'm not finished with you yet." But Rob was determined not to be surprised in the room by his mother.

They danced closely until one o'clock, trading passionate kisses. Rob tried to block out thoughts of Alana that kept creeping in. He wasn't sure if what he'd done was wrong or not.

It was easy to check on his mother, as Mrs. Ethan was dancing with every man at the party. At least she wasn't driven by booze tonight, he thought.

Finally Wendy's parents called her to come. Rob walked her to the lobby, and they kissed for a while in an alcove as her parents went to get the car. A black Lincoln stopped in front of the doors, its wipers moving quickly in a downpour.

"I can't believe you're going home tomorrow," Wendy said sadly.

"I know," said Rob. He felt attached to this girl.

"I'll call you in the morning."

"That would sure be nice. Maybe you can come visit," Rob said, sad at parting when they seemed so taken with one another.

"You live so far away." She kissed him on the cheek and made a dash for the car.

Before Rob went to bed he wrote her the poem she'd asked for. Perhaps, he thought, he'd mail it to Wendy from the airport.

Beating din of rain drops drumming
Heavy heart, lost the loving

Watch the stars in the sky
Never, ever be so high

Gone forever, empty being
Hollow world, never seeing

Your beautiful smile, your warm embrace
Your soft touch and shining face

Daggers deep, pain severe
Your sweet voice, never to hear

Chapter 32

Monday night Rob went to sleep early, tired out from the wedding and travel. He'd just shut off his bedroom light when he heard a hard knock on his bedroom door.

"Rob, phone," his father called irritably.

Rob shuffled to the kitchen, pulling on his bathrobe as he went.

"Hey man, what's up?" said the caller.

"Julius?

"Yeah." The voice was faint.

"What happened with you on Friday, eh?"

"Sorry, dude. Things are pretty bad."

"What do you mean, bad?"

"I can't do it any more," he quavered.

"Do what?" said Rob, confused. Was Julius quitting school?

"I'm useless, man. I screwed up your weekend like I fuck up everything."

Julius sounded stoned. "Julius, forget about it. It doesn't matter about Friday."

"It's no use, man. I know I'm a piece of shit. I'm going to end it and stop screwing everything up. This is it."

Rob stood up, his legs felt weak. "Where are you?"

"My place."

"Is your roommate there?"

"No, he left."

"Well, can you call someone else?"

"I don't know anyone else. I told you, Rob, I'm a complete fuck-up."

Rob's mind raced. "Is there a hospital you can go to?"

"No, Rob. No more hospitals," Julius whimpered.

"Do you have a doctor?"

"They're no help. Listen to me – it's over. I'm fucked, man."

Rob felt desperate. "Look, Julius, you aren't thinking straight, because of the drugs. Just don't do anything stupid. You need to find help."

"I can't be helped any more. I need to end it."

"Julius, that's silly, man."

"Everything is settled. I feel calm now."

Julius hung up. Rob's heart leaped and he dialled Julius' number. Julius had made threats before, but this sounded serious. But Julius' voice had never sounded so weak before, or so tranquil.

The phone rang five, ten, twenty times.

Rob waited ten minutes and called back. Still no answer. He called again.

Agitated, Rob dialled zero.

"Could you please connect me to an operator in British Columbia?"

"One moment."

"BC Tel. How can I help you?"

"Could you connect me to emergency in Vancouver? Nine-one-one, or whatever it is there? I have a friend in trouble."

"One moment."

There was a click and another lady said, "Emergency."

"Hello, my friend may be suicidal and it's possible he's overdosed, I don't know – he didn't sound good on the phone. But I'm calling long distance; can you get someone there to check on him?"

"We can dispatch an ambulance. Your friend's name and address, please?"

Rob unfolded the paper from his wallet. "Julius Stein, 632 West Georgia Street, apartment 302." She clicked off and Rob waited. Then she came back on the line. "I dispatched an ambulance. Please give me your name and phone number?"

He did.

"Are you next of kin?"

"No, a friend. How long till someone's there?"

"Ten minutes."

Rob hung up and dialled Julius' number. For the next hour he phoned every ten minutes. If the ambulance people had entered the apartment, they were not answering the phone. After an hour, he went through the process of connecting with the BC 911 operator again.

"Emergency."

"Hello, this is Rob Ethan. I called for an ambulance to West Georgia Street to check on my friend, Julius Stein. Did the ambulance get there yet?"

"Are you family, sir?"

"No, a friend."

"Sorry, I can't help you."

"But I'm the one who called for the ambulance. Can't you tell me what happened?"

"I'm sorry, please have someone in his family call and we'll direct them to the appropriate hospital or the police department."

"Why the police?"

"The police handle these matters, sir."

Rob put the phone down and stood for a moment, then dialled Julius' parents. No answer.

He watched TV and waited, bothered by swirling thoughts. Had he overreacted by calling 911? But what if he hadn't and something had happened?

He went into a half-sleep. There was Julius standing on a bridge, standing on the edge, leaning over. A train was coming. Get off the bridge Julius, he tried to scream, but his voice was frozen into a hoarse whisper.

He jerked awake. It was 1:00 a.m. in Vancouver, so he tried Julius' phone again. Perhaps he was home now, sleeping off the drugs.

He let the phone ring twenty times then he tried the Steins again.

"Who's this?"

"Mrs. Stein, it's Rob. Julius' friend."

"What's wrong?" she said sleepily.

"Julius called here last night around eleven. He didn't sound good. You know what I mean, right? After that, I kept trying his apartment, but there was no answer. I was worried, so I had an ambulance sent to his apartment."

"Jesus. What happened?"

"They won't tell me anything because I'm not a relative. So you need to call the police or hospital or something."

"Yes, yes, I'll try to wake Julius' father."

Chapter 33

Everything was closed the next day as a February snowstorm blew through the city. Every few hours Rob dialled a phone number hoping Julius would be home or the Steins could tell him something. But no one answered.

Now daylight was fading and the house lights were flicking on. Rob couldn't stay still any more. He slid on his parka and laced up his snow boots.

All he could see was a massive white expanse of blowing snow around the houses; the sidewalks and streets were gone. He wrapped his scarf around this face and started digging away at the heap of heavy snow on the veranda.

Heavy winds blasted fine snow into his eyes and back in the area that he had just cleared. Working at a breathless pace, he persevered until a narrow path led from the house to the city sidewalk, although it was going to partly fill back up.

After an hour, Rob came inside. He changed his sweaty shirt while his hot chocolate heated. His ears thawed and stung as he sipped the chocolate and watched the second hand sweep around the kitchen clock's face.

Time to dial again. Still no answer at Julius', so he called the Steins.

"Hello?" The cracking voice was Mrs. Stein's.

"It's Rob. Any news?"

"We don't know anything for sure."

"What do you mean, for sure? Did they find Julius?"

"No," she paused. "Some of his things."

"Where?"

"A park by the ocean, a few blocks from his apartment. They found his wallet and other personal items."

"What items?"

"Jacket and boots. His wallet was in his boots." Her voice broke.

"I don't get it. Did they find Julius?"

"No. They said it's possible that he went into the water."

"Into the water?"

"He may have gone into the water," Mrs. Stein repeated.

The picture of Julius walking into the ocean sank in.

After a mutual silence, Mrs. Stein offered, "I'll call you if I hear anything further," and hung up.

Rob called Julius' apartment again, but there was no one there.

Chapter 34

Rob couldn't find out anything more. He even tried calling the Steins and Julius' apartment before school Wednesday morning.

During English class his mind drifted to back to Julius. Damn, he thought, just when things had settled down with his mother. His marks from first term had been just below average and he knew he needed to do better.

Alana joined him in the student lounge after class.

"That was quite a storm last night," she commented. "My father isn't used to driving in these wild Canadian winters, and we barely made it to school this morning."

"This has been a bad year."

"Maybe it will get better."

"I doubt it." Rob had barely looked up.

"Are you referring to the weather or something else?"

Rob stirred his plastic spoon around in his coffee. "Nothing."

"You never come out with it, do you? If something's not right, you might as well tell me. Was your mother back to her old ways at the wedding?"

That was a sharp comment, thought Rob. He didn't say anything and stared down.

"Sorry, I didn't mean to be hurtful," she said apologetically.

"Not my mom this time, Alana, it's Julius."

"Mr. Longhair again! I thought the drug addict had straightened out."

Another cruel comment. Julius really irked her. Why couldn't she be more sensitive? "Well, he hasn't. I'm not even sure he's alive."

"What are you talking about?"

"I was supposed to go out with him Friday night, but when I called his place his roommate didn't know where he was. Then, on Monday, I get this call at home from Julius, talking like he wanted to kill himself and all. It was nuts."

"I'm sure he'll be OK. Surely he wouldn't do something stupid."

"No one's been able to find him for two days. Does it sound like he's OK?"

"Relax, mate, you worry too much. Julius is probably fine – maybe he needed some space or something."

"Maybe." It was tempting to agree with Alana. Julius hadn't gone too far before, just far enough to cry for help.

"So how was Vancouver, anyway?"

Wendy's face appeared before him. "I had a pretty fun time."

"Really! Did you behave?" Alana teased confidently.

"What do you mean, exactly, by behave?" He felt his face reddening.

"Did all the girls ask you to dance?" she asked coyly.

Rob chuckled, "Just one, actually," feeling he could dish out barbs, too.

"Really! And was that all it was, dancing?"

"It really didn't mean anything to me. It was just one night."

"You mean you actually slept with this girl?" Her smile melted away.

"No, it wasn't like that exactly … Alana, please…"

"Don't 'please' me, Rob. You can piss off!" she said, gathering her things. Off she marched.

He sat frozen in the brown lounge chair, his mind spinning, wondering how he had managed to make a mess of everything.

That evening Rob just lay on the couch, staring at the television. He hadn't been able to eat the dinner his father had made. One moment the argument with Alana would rerun in his head and the next moment he would worry about Julius.

Just before eleven, the phone rang. Father and son looked at each other, wondering about the late call.

"I'll get it." Mr. Ethan said, rising from his easy chair.

Finally, maybe some news, Rob thought.

"Rob, it's Mr. Stein."

Relieved, Rob jogged to the phone in the kitchen.

"They found him," Julius' father said in a slurred voice.

"Great! Where?"

"No, I said they found him," Julius' father said more loudly.

A pause.

"They found his body today about two miles from the park in the water."

Rob hung up and fell into the kitchen chair.

Chapter 35

It surprised Rob how heavy the coffin was when they carried it out to the hearse after the funeral. When Julius' mother had asked, Rob had agreed to be a pallbearer, though he was unsure he'd be able to carry out the duties properly, having never been to a funeral before.

The only people at the funeral were a few relatives and Rob. Julius' mother shook and cried, wiping her eyes with a white handkerchief, but his father wore a blank face.

Julius' uncle from Winnipeg read the eulogy. Mostly he focused on Julius' childhood accomplishments in Cubs and gymnastics and on his painting. But he also mentioned the difficulties of Julius' teenage years, and said that though Julius' family had loved him and tried to understand him, they had not always been able to help him.

As Rob sat in the black limo on the way back to the Steins' residence, he wished he could see Julius one more time, to hear him talk about a painting or taunt him with a racy comment about Alana. So this is what it's like when someone dies, he thought. A continuous surprise that they're not there, doing the things that only they do.

Exams were looming. After the funeral Rob had tried with more or less success to focus his mind on his schoolwork. Now he sat at his desk, staring at his textbook, hearing meltwater dripping from the eaves, trying to cram information into his head. He had saved this whole Sunday for studying, but images of Julius kept coming between his eyes and the page.

He was wasting his time, he decided. So he made a cup of coffee and put it on his nightstand, propped two pillows up against the headboard of his bed and crawled under his comforter. Next to the steaming mug was the Alcoholics Anonymous book he had taken from his mother's months ago.

Two hours had passed before he reached for his coffee, now cold. Rob adjusted his pillow and thought about what the book said. Maybe he wasn't so different from everyone else. Lots of other people had problems and feelings like his.

If he was having feelings like the people in the book, should he think of his life as "unmanageable," as the book insisted? He wasn't sure his life was out of control. His mother's drinking and Julius' depression were much bigger problems.

Still, he had been affected by their problems, as Bud had once pointed out. He worried about other people in a way that left him miserable with responsibility and guilt. That was his problem. And he had to ask – had all his worry made his mother stop drinking? Had his worrying saved Julius?

"Rob, Alana's on the phone," called his dad.

"I just found out about Julius, Rob. Why didn't you tell me?"

"You weren't talking to me."

"Yes, well, that was about a different issue. Anyhow, I'm sorry about making things worse for you."

"I'm sorry too, about the Vancouver thing. It just kind of happened."

"I suppose I hadn't any right to be upset. We'd only been on a handful of dates."

"Well, we both see it the same way," Rob asserted.

"It's possible I may be willing to get past this."

"That would be super. Will you start by coming with me to the Lawren Harris exhibit next Saturday?" He had a special reason for asking her to join him on Saturday.

"Who's Harris?"

"Landscape painter in the Group of Seven, Julius told me about him." Rob paused, realizing he had spoken as if Julius were still living.

"I'd love to, but I have a biology exam the Monday after. My worst subject. I need to cram all weekend."

Disappointed, he wondered if that was an excuse. "Well, see you next week at class, unless you want to do something tonight, maybe?"

"Thanks, but I'm going to the ballet with my parents. *Romeo and Juliet.*"

Rob said in a melodramatic voice, "Romeo, Romeo, wherefore art thou Romeo?"

"It's a ballet, silly," Alana giggled. "She won't say that."

Rob realized his faux pas. So what, he'd been having fun. "She'll pirouette for him, then. You said you used to do ballet – I'd like to see you try that."

"We'll see. Goodbye, now."

Chapter 36

☷ Wow, thought Rob, this looked like the work Julius used to do! The painting was of a single cloud hiding the setting sun. The white-and-grey cloud was shaped like a croissant. The sky was turning blue-black, but the sun cast a pale yellow shimmer on the water below.

Beside the picture there was a plaque that said *Clouds, Lake Superior, 1923.* As he wandered through the rest of the gallery, he became convinced that Julius had practised by imitating Harris.

The discovery made Julius seem closer, as if he might suddenly appear, joking and teasing. But then, when he left the gallery, Rob felt even sadder than before. Some eighteenth birthday.

As he rode home on the bus, the sky was nearly dark and the streets were empty. Tiny droplets from a spring shower made slivers on the bus window. Rarely did it rain on his birthday, March 19. Only once before could he remember a birthday rain, maybe for his eighth birthday.

His father had come home from work early that day, so that when his mother came home they could go right out for a special dinner. They were celebrating at a restaurant just for him. He changed to his best pants and button-up shirt. And his tooled leather cowboy boots – they were too small, but they looked great and they made him tall. He sat on his bed to wait, ignoring the aching toes.

But then he heard yelling. "Where the Christ were you? We're going out for Rob's birthday!"

"So I forgot. I'm sorry."

Rob opened his door a crack.

"Sorry isn't good enough. How could you not remember?"

"You and Rob aren't the only things that matter to me, you know. I got supreme hell at work from Harry and needed to unwind."

"You mean you needed to get pissed. You're disgusting."

"Screw you!" shouted his mother.

By this time Rob had covered his head with his pillow. After a few minutes his dad had come to his door.

"Look, buddy, here's a sandwich I made for you and a piece of birthday cake."

Rob had eaten the sandwich, but left the cake on his dresser. Then he fell asleep in his clothes and boots. He couldn't bring himself to take them off, in case it wasn't too late to go out for his birthday.

His mother had left home for a month after that night. Rob had felt that his birthday had caused all the trouble. If they hadn't had plans for him, his mother would not have drunk, his parents would not have fought and his mother would not have left.

Rob snapped out of the memory with a stomach ache. The rain now raced in sheets across the bus window and he couldn't see a thing outside. The pounding on the metal roof of the bus drowned out the engine. Rob found it a sad sound.

His feet and ankles would have felt the cold first, thought Rob. But Julius must have kept walking, letting himself be engulfed by the water. Then his clothes must have begun to weigh him down, until there was no turning back.

What could he have been feeling during the last moments? Had he wanted to die so much he didn't even struggle? The idea was horrible to Rob. His arms grew heavy and his legs and back felt frozen to the seat of the bus. He felt immobilized by a tremendous weight.

The rain had tapered to single-drop paths on the window. As Rob lurched up the aisle at his stop, his reflection in the window seemed to have long trails of water streaming from his eyes down his cheeks.

He wiped his face with his sleeve and got off the bus.

Chapter 37

Sensei was watching and Rob knew he had to focus if he was to be chosen for his black belt test in the summer. The last two *katas* were fast, at full speed. His mind had been wandering during class – he kept envisioning Julius' coffin in the funeral home. He gave himself a deep breath.

"*Dan Kumite,* pair up with a partner," Sensei commanded from the front of the dojo.

In this exercise the attacker launched preset punches and kicks and his opponent defended with preset counterstrikes. Although each opponent knew what strike was coming, he couldn't anticipate its timing, speed or ferocity.

Rob paired with Kevin Baker, who was about his height and build but a higher rank. Kevin would be tested for *shodan,* his first black belt ranking, within the next few weeks.

The two opponents bowed ceremoniously to one another, and then Rob fixed his gaze on Kevin's eyes. He dropped his right arm to deliver a punch at Kevin's chest, shooting it out like an arrow and tensing his entire body at the last moment to deliver maximum force, as Sensei had shown them. Kevin blocked the punch and returned with a kick at Rob's midsection, but before the foot reached its target Rob circled his arm and deflected the attack, spinning Kevin around.

Full of steam, Rob launched a second punch at Kevin's chest.

Hit him, penetrate his defences, Rob told himself. But Kevin blocked the punch and aimed to punch low on Rob's ribs. Rob again blocked, causing Kevin to pull his arm away and rub it to diffuse the pain.

Now it was time for the second set. Rob threw a punch at Kevin's chest. Try to score with this one, he said inwardly. Harder, more relaxed. His knuckles met Kevin's chest muscle and his hand sunk into Kevin's body. Rob's arm was knocked away with a circle block, but too late to stop the strike. Then, when Kevin counterpunched towards Rob's midsection, Rob dropped his arm down like an axe chopping a log. It was a heavy blow to Kevin's arm and he grimaced.

Kevin now threw a higher punch, but Rob blocked it. Then his rear leg sprang up and he buried his toes into Kevin's stomach. Right on, he thought, as Kevin doubled over in pain.

When the *kumite* was over Rob changed out of his gi into his regular clothes. As he took the stairs down to the street two at a time, the high from the hard workout started to dissipate.

Loser. Why hadn't he done more to help Julius?

He took five steps towards Main Street, then stopped and walked resolutely back in the opposite direction towards the bus stop.

Rotten life, stinking world, worthless person.

He turned back towards Main Street, looking for something to drive the thoughts away. His pace picked up; he sidestepped a pile of broken beer bottles in a puddle of vomit.

He arrived at Main Street and gazed up and down it. A street person staggered into him and weaved on past. Rob sauntered down the street and into a pinball arcade and pool hall.

After he had played a while, two teenagers and an older, hefty guy with a pockmarked face surrounded him and watched him play the last ball.

"You got a smoke?" one of the teens asked.

"Nope."

The ball went down the middle and the game was over.

"How about a quarter so we can play?" the same boy asked Rob.

"All out, sorry," Rob said and turned to leave.

"How about a buck, then." The kid stood between Rob and the door.

"I told you, I haven't got any money," Rob said calmly.

"Then why don't you open your wallet and show me?" the kid said, tapping him on the shoulder.

"Piss off," said Rob, stepping quickly around the boy and out the door. The boys followed and Rob readied for trouble.

The hefty older guy walked past Rob and turned around, blocking his way. "You weren't nice to my friends in there, and it's going to cost you ten bucks."

Rob looked up at the older guy flanked by the teenagers. "I told the truth; I haven't got money." When the older guy reached for Rob's pocket to take out his wallet, Rob blocked his arm.

But then two boys grabbed Rob's arms and one got an arm around Rob's throat, choking him. The older guy took Rob's wallet out of his pocket and withdrew a ten.

"Liar, you deserve a beatin'."

Attack, thought Rob. He stomped down as hard as he could on the toe of the boy whose arm was around his neck and ripped his elbow into the kid's gut.

A kick cracked Rob in the ribs, a fist came hurling at his face. Rob blocked and counterpunched, smashing the older guy in the jaw, kicking the first kid in the gut and sending a right fist into the eye of the other. He sucked hard to catch his breath.

The older guy recovered, grabbed Rob's hair from behind and put him in a headlock. Now he was really in trouble. Everything started to fade as he gasped helplessly for air. He thought he might die.

A voice seemed to be roaring at them from a distance, but the older guy only choked Rob harder and started punching him in the face.

The guy's arm suddenly released Rob's neck – someone was fighting on Rob's side. Rob wheeled, coughing and gasping, and saw Sensei. He must have followed Rob to Main Street.

The older guy swung at Sensei's head and Sensei blocked his arm, simultaneously chopping behind his attacker's ear to knock him out. Sensei caught him on the way down and laid him out on the sidewalk, and the teens disappeared.

Rob was ready to leave the guy, but Sensei dropped to his knees and worked over him until he came to.

"Here's your wallet. Let's go."

"Thanks," Rob muttered.

"Not sure you need so much real-life practice, eh?"

"Sorry."

"You head home and put ice on your face. We'll talk about it another time."

Chapter 38

It was a restless night for Rob. He worried that his throbbing jaw was broken. Even more painful was the memory of being rescued by Sensei Sonberg. How could he face his teacher?

Dawn found him at his desk with a coffee, struggling to concentrate on Descartes. The philosophy final was in three days and nothing was sinking in. He put his forehead down on the desk.

Over the last few months he had driven hard to improve his studies and karate forms. He had allowed hardly any time for loafing and felt lousy when he tried to relax. Now he found he could no longer push dark thoughts out of his mind. Julius' final desperate act played over and over.

Could he reach the point of embracing his own death? It might be possible, Rob feared, for him to go down a similar path of despair. He knew how the weight of self-blame for misery in one's world could feel unbearable. Death would relieve this kind of suffering.

He lay on his bed and stared at the ceiling, and childhood memories floated to him. His drunken mother making everyone's life insane. The endless screaming tirades … his desperation to hide his secret … the isolation that it had brought from friends and family. Life with his mother's addiction had been like living on a tight rope, swaying back and forth with her crazy life, always afraid of falling off.

The only good thing to come from this, he decided, was inner strength. At Julius' funeral while the family had cried, Rob had just watched. As in most things, he had been an observer, and not a participant.

But had closing the door to pain made him unable to open the door to feelings, as Bud had warned? Had his strength killed his emotions?

He had chosen this path because he thought it was safe – but maybe it wasn't so safe. Rob turned memories over and over in his mind, playing the worst scenes like movies. The self-destructiveness of his path was obvious.

Rob pulled the covers up to his chin like a security blanket. For the first time in his life the violent storm had calmed and he had nothing to hide from. Freed from chaos, he was empty.

There must be another path, he thought. One that would let him cry over Julius, grieve the difficult years with his mother, have a natural smile instead of a forced one.

It seemed as though a door was ajar and all he had to do was open it. Now he knew he wanted not only to survive, but also to see the sun, to feel the wind and to smell the air.

If there was a force of renewal building inside him, he would test it. He would take the first step on this new path and see where it led him.

Rob picked up the handset and dialled Bud's number with sweaty palms. And hung up. After two minutes of staring at the phone, he dialled again and squashed the impulse to hang up after the first ring. He had no idea what he was going to say.

"Bud, it's Rob. Am I calling too early?"

"Not at all. Did you call a minute ago?"

"Yes. Sorry I hung up."

"That's OK! Good to hear from you; it's been a while. How are you making out?"

"Rough with exams and all."

"Lots of work?"

"Yeah."

"How're you feeling?"

"Not great."

"The last couple of months have been lousy, huh? How about I pick you up and we grab breakfast?"

"That would be good."

Rob stood by the door and waited.

After a few minutes the Mercedes pulled up. Rob extended his hand as they met in the driveway. "Hi, Bud." But Bud wrapped both arms around the young man and hugged him so tightly his leather coat squeaked.

"It's good to see you, Rob. I think maybe I needed to see you as much as you needed to see me."

"Really?"

"Hey, you know how much Jeannie and I love you and your Mom."

Warmth flushed over Rob's face and chest. He could not recall anyone saying something like that to him before. It felt like someone else's clothes.

"What happened to your chin?"

"It's a long story, I'll tell you over breakfast."

"I'll hold you to that. Where to?"

"Sal's Diner. I'm starved."

"On our way," said Bud backing out of the driveway. The sun was rising, but when Rob looked back at the house, it still sat in long, dark shadows from the trees.

Bud hit the gas and they sped away.

Chapter 39

Rob peered about for the waitress, eager to eat at once. The aroma of bacon and eggs floated in the air and red lamps warmed plates of food at the far end of the lunch counter. Rob and Bud took a booth in the row along the window wall opposite the counter.

A middle-aged waitress in a soiled white apron walked over with a coffee pot in her hand.

"Coffee, gentlemen?"

They turned over their coffee cups and she filled each up with the steaming black liquid.

Rob shook some sugar out of the shaker and passed it to Bud.

"No, just black for me, young man."

Rob stared down into his cup.

"Glad you called, we need to talk about Julius," Bud said, as he sopped up slopped coffee with a serviette.

"I wanted to avoid that." Rob directed his gaze out the window.

"I know, we haven't seen you in a long time. You've immersed yourself in school, you haven't gone out, it seems you're trying to stay very busy."

"Lots of work and exams, karate and everything else."

"Maybe, but you need to get over Julius' death. You haven't grieved, you haven't started to feel the loss you suffered."

"Ya know, maybe it's best just to put that behind me and move on." Rob's voice was weak.

"Well, I think you need to talk about it." Bud sounded like he meant business.

"I guess."

"Julius was your closest friend. He was a very warm and bright young man, just that he couldn't escape his demons. It's normal and healthy to let yourself feel pain and sorrow."

"I find it best not think about things like that."

"Rob, let me ask you an important question."

"Fine, shoot." Rob picked up his coffee cup and took a gulp.

"If you don't feel sadness then how do you expect to feel happiness?"

"What do you mean?"

"If you've learned to turn off all the things that have hurt you in life, do you think you can turn on happiness or joy without getting stuck? Without feeling sorrow, sadness or other emotions, you can't expect to feel happy about anything either. I don't think I have seen you laugh once. The two go hand in hand."

Rob stared at Bud in silence, wanting to protest, but could find no words.

"You have to admit that you have some work to do on yourself. You need to accept that you have not had an easy life. Losing your mother for most of your life was tough and you survived because you had inner strength of character. But you paid a price, Rob. You sacrificed a part of yourself to survive."

"Well, it's how I got by."

"Absolutely. Those defence mechanisms kept you going in an alcoholic's home, but those coping methods are going to hinder you from reaching your full potential as an adult. Your ability to have a healthy relationship with a woman, with your children or in a career are at risk because of your family situation."

Alana's criticisms flashed into Rob's thoughts. What Bud was saying seemed to ring true.

Bud put his coffee down on the table and his face was serious. "You have to stop blaming yourself or feeling that you are some way responsible for all the bad things that happened to you. Your mother's drinking, Julius' death, your parent's divorce, were not your doing. You were innocent, just caught up in other people's problems. It was not your stuff, but became yours by default."

Rob sat stoned-faced, listening intently, looking out the window, thinking about his life.

"You assumed the role of a parent and mediator as a child. You believed you could control or cure the problem, but it was not within your power to do so. You suffered pain as a result. Your spirit was dampened. Now you need to learn how to forgive yourself and move on with your own life. There are ways to cope with your past."

"I really don't know what to do."

"For starters, you have to acknowledge that your behaviour and emotions were shaped by your childhood. This is accepting the reality of your past. Then you are going to have to grieve the loss of your childhood. Just start talking about things that happened in the past and what's bothering you. Isolation is a symptom of the problem. You can't carry the weight of the world all on your own shoulders. I learned that a long time ago. You know, before I sold my company, I drank to kill the fear and insecurity I had about every little problem that came up. I didn't think I was smart or savvy enough to make it. Being rich and successful was what I wanted more than anything in life, but the harder I worked towards that goal the worse things became."

"Really?"

"Yes, really, Rob. I drank because it numbed my feelings of

insecurity and the lack of self-worth. I became financially successful despite my addiction, but inside, I still felt like a failure. I worried myself sick over everything. I tried to control everything that happened. I manipulated people to do what I wanted them to do. I was scared every time an employee went in a direction that I didn't want them to go in. I often fired them on the spot. I was terrified of mistakes in business or in life."

"That sounds familiar," Rob said, staring into Bud's warm eyes.

"Good, let me continue for a moment. If an important customer called me to complain about a manufacturing defect or flaw, I was a basket case. To avoid a problem in our product line I drove my staff and myself to near breakdown. I couldn't face the idea of having unhappy customers or trying to explain why things weren't exactly as they had ordered. I lay awake many nights worrying about every possible thing that could go wrong."

"I worry all the time too," Rob admitted, wanting to connect with the discussion.

"In my case I worried if I had enough money to meet payroll. I worried if the colour of our fabrics were going to run. I always worried whether the bank would call my loan when I went over my credit line. Booze addressed all those problems – for a while, anyway. They went away when I drank and my mind was so scrambled from the alcohol that I didn't have the capacity to worry or fret about things."

"Doesn't sound like a lot of fun," Rob replied.

"It wasn't, but I had to hit bottom before I got help. My drinking got worse and my first wife left me. I almost lost the business. The tax department was breathing down my back, I was in bad shape, but I got help."

"I didn't realize you went through all that. I mean, you were very successful and all that."

"I hid my problems very well. My main preoccupation was to make people think that I was a successful, happy business executive. I played the part exceedingly well, but inside, I knew I was a fraud, so I never showed people the real me. But I want to focus on you for a moment."

The bacon and eggs arrived.

"Need anything else here, gentleman?" The waitress started flipping through a stack of checks, looking for the right one.

"I'll take that and a refill on the coffee, please." Bud looked at Rob, waiting for the waitress to leave. She handed him the bill and he put it down by his plate.

"Rob, if you had the opportunity to change anything about your life, what would it be?"

Rob had to swallow a lump. "I guess to be happy."

"It's all about that, isn't it?" Bud said in a reassuring tone.

"I just don't know how to get there." He felt close to tears.

"Every person on this earth is trying to figure that out, you are not alone." Bud said, and slurped his coffee.

"Well, how did you do it?"

Bud chuckled. "How do you know I am happy?"

"It just looks like you are. You seem so content with everything, you know, like nothing bothers you."

"That's true most of the time. I practice a lot of gratitude about life."

"That's exactly where I have a problem, I never have anything to be grateful for." Rob bit off the end of a strip of bacon and wiped his finger on the serviette.

"It's true you had a difficult childhood and this year has been complete hell, but that's not really what I'm talking about."

Confused by that comment, Rob sat back in the booth and folded his arms.

"Gratitude is just a tool in life. It doesn't mean that there are not lousy things around you. The world will always have suffering in it. But you need to constantly remind yourself over and over that there are many things in life to be grateful for. You know, every time I see someone with a life-threatening illness, I realize that there could be larger challenges than what I have had to face. They never seem to begrudge their situation. So why should I? Think about the millions of starving and homeless people in the world. Think about their suffering. Your life may not be so bad in comparison. Be grateful for what you have in life, good food, clothes and a roof over your head, a fine education, parents who really love you. That's a lot. Every time you do anything find a little something to be grateful for. Do that all day long, it works."

"I am grateful for this piece of bacon," Rob said with a chuckle, holding it up before stuffing it in his mouth.

"That's a good start, but don't stop there." Bud laughed too. "And don't worry about everything. I have one very important thing I always say to myself."

"What's that?"

"Don't worry about something until you have something to worry about."

"I think I get it."

"Well, people always drive themselves crazy worrying about what might or could happen. Just wait and see. Nine times out of ten it doesn't happen, or if it does, it's not nearly as bad as it seemed beforehand."

The waitress reappeared, filled Bud's coffee cup and cleared the empty plates.

"Getting back to my main point, you need to open up more, especially about Julius and the things in your life that were difficult. You can't hide forever. Talk about your problems with someone, talk to God or your Higher Power. It really doesn't matter, just try to draw strength and comfort from something greater and more powerful than yourself."

"How about a dragon?"

Chapter 40

Early the next morning Rob drifted in and out of sleep. The curtains fluttered in the soft wind. The morning light, filtered through the trees, peeped between the curtains and cast dancing glints of gold into the dusky bedroom. Slowly, the fluid forms took the shape of a shadowy dragon performing a *kata* on the ceiling.

Layers of Rob's body seemed to peel off and float upward. They were old lives, lifting from his body and being consumed by the dragon. His body grew lighter.

The dragon drifted down to hover above Rob, and a shadowy mist seeped into Rob's body below his navel. Energy grew in his abdomen and travelled up his spine like steam rising through a pipe. The force reached his head and grew warmer. Then the dragon emerged and sat atop his body like a lookout.

Rob stared at the ceiling and wondered what he had seen. Had it been real, or just a dream? Did it matter? His usual morning heaviness was gone; instead he felt full of energy.

By 10:30 Alana was honking her horn outside the house. Passing the hallway mirror, he noticed his jaw now had an oval black bruise.

"Nice to see you, sweetie," Alana said as he climbed in.

"You too." She looked splendid with her golden hair in a

ponytail. A light scent of her perfume filled the Buick.

She looked at him. "What in hell happened to you?"

"I'll tell you while we eat. It's a long story." Rob leaned towards Alana and kissed her.

"Hey, I wasn't expecting that," she mumbled through a return kiss.

"Hell, I thought I'd try it out and see if you smacked me."

"I wouldn't hit your chin; it looks sore."

"I'm safe to keep going, then?"

"Too much further and I'll hit you somewhere else!" she said and they laughed together. For the first time, Rob noticed something artificial in his laugh. He thought about what Bud had said the day before – if you don't let yourself feel sorrow, how deep do you think your happiness is going to be?

"By the way, where are we going?"

"Let's go to Sal's," Rob suggested, drawn back to the place where he and Bud had talked. "Well, how did your test go?"

"I studied so hard, but I'm not sure I did that well."

"You did your best, so there's no sense worrying about it now," said Rob, surprising himself. "I almost flunked chemistry last year. Science isn't my thing either."

When they arrived at the restaurant, Rob led Alana to the booth he and Bud had shared the morning before.

"Rob, before we eat I have to tell you something."

"What's that?" Was she going to dump him for someone else?

"Next week my parents and I are going to England for the summer."

Right when a romance was about to blossom between them, she was going to leave. "If I proposed, would you marry me and stay here?" Rob offered, only half-joking.

"First I'll have to see the diamond!"

"We can break into Bell Jewellers and you can have your pick."

"How romantic."

"Seriously, though. I thought we had been getting along lately."

"I've had a thing for you, Rob. But you've never made much effort in my direction."

That stunned Rob. "I didn't realize that's what you thought."

"You don't realize a lot about people, do you?"

Rob didn't say anything. Had he really missed her signals?

"You don't open up at all – I have to drag things out of you. I was completely amazed when you showed a hint of affection in the auto."

"I suppose I'm a rookie at romance," he said, looking off.

"You've never fallen for someone before?"

"Well, yes." He struggled to say more, but words wouldn't come.

"So would you say you feel strongly about me?" she quizzed him.

Rob stared into Alana's eyes. "Yeah, you know."

"No, I *don't* know."

"I could try to be more open."

"Try like this," she said, and leaned forward so their lips met. "So are you going to visit me in England?"

"Yeah, right." Rob shook his head. She was probably trying to cheer him up.

"You could stay with us, then all you'd need was plane fare."

"Are you serious?" A wave of excitement washed over Rob as he thought about how great a trip to England would be.

"Of course. I know some romantic spots," she said. "We could have a fantastic time."

"Now you're leading me on." Rob wagged his finger.

"So I am."

Then he remembered that, in any case, he still hadn't landed a summer job and his bank account presently held less than a hundred bucks, and his excitement crashed.

"No can do," he said. "I just don't have the money."

Chapter 41

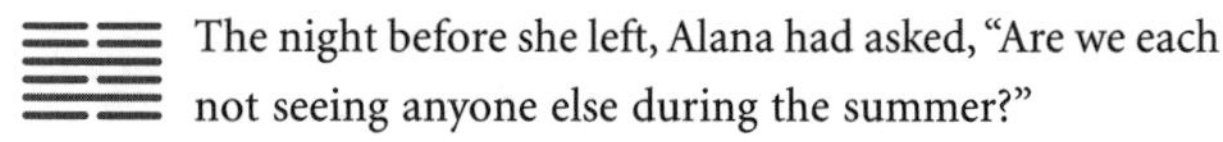

The night before she left, Alana had asked, "Are we each not seeing anyone else during the summer?"

"As in dating other people?" he murmured, thinking of his encounter with Wendy in Vancouver.

"That's my question, mate."

"What about you?"

"Yes, I've a few blokes at home that would like to see me," she said teasingly.

Rob's face flushed and he looked away. "That kinda hurts." He could never decide if she really wanted him.

"Rob, I just want to know where I stand. You need to tell me. I wouldn't be asking if I didn't care."

The next day Rob moped around the house with England on his mind. He couldn't see any way around the money problem.

He sat at the kitchen table staring at the cup of coffee. OK, he thought, this is real pain. Emotion swept over him like ocean waves washing gently on the beach. He wanted to go deeper, to let the water cover his body.

An image of Julius lying unconscious in the water appeared. He pushed that image away and instead imagined that he was floating with Alana in his arms. They sank until they hit the riverbed. When their lungs felt like they were going to explode they swam to the surface. But when he came up, Alana was gone. Black clouds had descended and he knew his bliss had been an illusion.

This was too much, he thought. He'd better halt his slipping mood, put up the pain barriers. But wasn't he tired of fighting? Maybe he could surrender and let the pain come. He watched the trees in the front yard sway in the wind. If only he could be like that, he thought, go with the wind.

Time to practice karate. He pushed back the large green upholstered chair in the living room and kicked off his slippers. First he worked on *Sanchin kata* and readied to begin his black belt *kata, Seisan.*

The sun was blazing through the window, and he made a whirling shadow that only caught his eye as he made his final move. The shadow was a dragon leaping in the air, with the arms moving in a circular swirl and the motion of its body full of spirit, the breath strong. It landed on the ground to take root in the earth, and he thought he felt his spirit fuse with it.

There it was, he thought. Something he could draw on. It was his protector and he didn't have to deal with life on his own any more. He could just live it – taking strength from this shadow of the dragon. In the open space of the living room, Rob stood with his feet rooted to the floor and his eyes wide, seeing everything.

The telephone broke the silence.

"Hi, honey."

"Mom, I was going to call you. I haven't heard from you lately."

"That's because I worked nights this week."

"How's the job going?"

"All I can say is I'm thankful to have it, because it's no fun to be poor. Maybe it'll lead to better things – the guys in production say I can proofread faster than anyone else. But enough about me. How are you doing?"

"OK."

"Just OK?"

"Alana's leaving for England today."

"So my baby is brokenhearted?"

"Kind of, I guess. We were getting along pretty well. She actually invited me to visit her in England."

"Why don't you go?"

"No cash. I'm still trying to nail down my landscaping job with the city."

There was a pause. "You wouldn't start work till next month, right?"

"Yes, that's when they hire."

"Listen, honey, I'll buy your ticket."

Rob was stunned. His mother hadn't been working that long. And even if she had the money, he didn't deserve such a huge gift.

"You can't spend all your money on me, Mom. You need it for yourself."

"I insist. Let me do this for you, Rob. Wouldn't it make you happy?"

"I guess so."

"I don't want to buy your love, but I have to find ways to say I am sorry for all I put you through. This can be the beginning."

The conversation felt unreal.

"Honey, please say yes. It'll hurt me if you don't."

OK then. "Thanks."

"Don't thank me, my God, son, don't thank me," her voice quivered and began to break up. "I owe you a hell of a lot more than a few hundred bucks. I owe you a hell of a lot more. Jesus, you just don't understand how much. That is the pity, you just don't realize it do you?" His mother cried softly and said she had to go.

Rob stood with the receiver, amazed at how many ways he was at a crossroads in his life.

Chapter 42

As Rob entered the dojo that afternoon, he was met by Sensei coming out of his small office.

"You look better," Sensei said with a half-smile. "Welcome back."

"Uh, sorry about missing class. I was pretty sore."

"Go get your gi on. We'll talk more later."

After warm-ups, Sensei told the students to perform the *Sanchin kata* in slow speed.

"*Rei,*" he commanded. The thirty students bowed to the front to demonstrate respect for Sensei and for the founder of karate.

"*Ichi.*"

The students drew back their arms and thrust them at an imaginary assailant, stepping forward. Their hands remained open as if the fingers were going to penetrate the attacker's chest.

"*Ni.*"

The students thrust with the other arm and stepped forward.

"*Muwate.*"

They turned to face a new threat from behind and thrust again. As Rob moved through the form, aware of his surroundings, the storm within his mind quieted as if he were in the eye of a hurricane. He experienced no thoughts, no fears and no distractions, no past and no future. He stood between the last moment and the next. His breath cycled energy through his body until spirit grew from the breath, fusing his mind and body. By the end, he felt the dragon moving out of his centre and enveloping him in a glowing oval of energy.

The soft joy of *kata* lingered past the final bow to Sensei. As he changed into his street clothes he felt as though nothing could ever bother him. If only the feeling would stay with him, he thought, as he headed for the stairs down to his other reality.

Sensei stopped him. "Sit, sit," he said, waving him to the wooden bench in his office. Rob sat, wiping the sweat from his brow.

"How's your jaw?"

"Still a little sore, but better."

"I have to decide whether you will be grading for black belt this summer."

"I know."

"What do you think should be the basis of my decision?"

"Uh, whether I have perfected my *kata*?"

"I'm not sure *kata* can be perfected," Sensei smiled. "But what else?"

"If I know my *bunkai* and *kumite?*"

"Yes, those are important. Is that all?"

Rob dreaded what was coming.

"What about being more serious?" said Sensei sternly.

"I can try to make classes more regularly," said Rob, dodging the point.

Sensei shook his head slowly. "I mean taking life seriously – deadly seriously – not as a hobby. Training as a warrior can make a difference between life and death."

Rob looked down.

"In a black belt candidate I am looking for a warrior's spirit above all else. That, by necessity, includes living with honour and pursuing correct moral conduct. Obtaining your black belt so you can indulge in an unnecessary fight is not the proper attitude of a warrior, Rob. Rather, you should consider training as a way of refining your inner spirit."

"I understand, Sensei."

"Good. Then let's not have any more trips down to Main Street."

Rob flushed and nodded.

Sensei smiled. "Though I admire your courage in mixing it up with three guys."

"It's a foolish kind of courage," said Rob sheepishly. "Thanks for helping me out of a bad situation."

"Oh, I don't think you are completely out of your situation yet."

Chapter 43

The buds had just given birth, and Rob sat on the lawn enjoying the sight of new leaves and the chirps of robins. It was warm for May, and wearing shorts and a T-shirt made him feel particularly free.

He was waiting for his mother. She had asked Rob to spend the day in the country with her before he flew out that evening. She could borrow Bud's car. Rob sensed her nervousness; it would be her first time at the wheel since the accident.

Eventually the big black Mercedes rolled down the street and stopped in front of the Ethans' house. Rob asked through the window, "How's the driving?"

"A little scary," she said, lighting a cigarette. A bright headband held her black hair from her face and she was wearing a red tie-on halter top.

"Do you want to stay around here?"

"No, I have to get back up on the horse, as they say. I'm saving up to have my own car again, though it won't be like this one."

Rob didn't answer. He felt guilty again for taking her money for the trip.

"Don't frown, honey. This is supposed to be a fun day. How about we drive out to the lake? We haven't been there since you were a little squirt."

As they drove out of the city, Rob thought of picnics at the lake with his parents. They'd eat their lunches on wooden tables by the shore, and then, after waiting exactly half an hour, Rob would dash into the water and dance around until he didn't feel the cold. Then he'd run to the woods to start a game of hide-and-seek with his father. Never with his mother, she didn't like the woods.

They passed through subdivisions to vast open farmland. When they passed a red barn and cattle right beside the road, Rob noticed his mother was missing the scenery entirely. She was gripping the wheel tightly, concentrating on the road.

For Rob, the drive seemed to wake up memories of happiness in his childhood. But where had it all gone? Maybe this was the day to screw up his courage and get some answers.

"Why did you start drinking, mom?"

Mrs. Ethan kept her stare fixed on the road, but she turned the radio down. "That's a long story, honey."

"So tell me about it, then."

"OK, you're asking for it," she said with a soft smile. "For starters, your grandfather died when I was young, as you know."

"In the war, right?"

"Yup. He was a paratrooper in the army and on D-Day at the end of the war his unit was dropped inland to help the troops coming off of the beaches. They were blown off course and as the men floated down, German troops picked them off before they hit the ground."

"So that's how grandpa died?"

"More or less. They said Dad's parachute got caught in a high tree and as he struggled to cut himself free he was machine gunned."

"I've never heard about that."

"Darn, I should have asked your uncle to show you his war

medals when we were in Vancouver," Mrs. Ethan said, her lighter shaking in her hand as she tried to light a fresh cigarette.

"After my brother told me that, I had nightmares of my father hanging and screaming from the big oak tree in front of our house. Afterwards I was always terrified to go into the woods."

Her voice shook. "When my dad didn't come back, neither did the love." Tears welled up in her eyes, so she pulled off onto the shoulder.

"Your grandmother married my stepfather – a miserable bastard. He was a salesman and went out on the road a lot. But when he was home, he and my mother drank and fought. He was a good-looking man and she accused him of keeping a lady in each town; she was probably right. My mother changed when she was with him – all she did was cry and shout. And my stepfather never really wanted us around, either."

"Boy, I didn't know any of this."

Mrs. Ethan took a deep breath, checked over her shoulder and pulled back onto the road.

"So me and your Uncle Tom, we hid from it. When we got into our teens, we poured ourselves booze from whiskey bottles in the living room bar and then topped them up with water. I doubt our stepdad ever got really drunk from that whisky, we diluted it so much," she said with a chuckle.

"When my brother got a little older he could buy homemade crabapple wine, so we'd sneak out to the back yard and drink ourselves silly. Mind you, he eventually stopped drinking, unlike some."

"But didn't you stop for a while after you met Dad?"

"For a while."

"What happened?" Rob felt like an interrogator, but he had to know.

"I lost a baby girl at birth a couple of years after you were born.

You would've had a sister."

Rob felt a large lump in his throat.

"We couldn't bear to try again, and that left a big hole in me. Drinking numbed the pain, but the more I drank the more I became ashamed of who I was, so I'd drink to deal with that. I guess the basic problem was I'd never loved myself, so I blamed myself for everything that happened, even the loss of my little girl."

"I didn't know that," said Rob sadly.

"Neither did I! I lived in denial. But after my car accident I more or less hit bottom and I realized I was going to die a lonely death. I realized I had to stop denying that I had come from a hard life and that it had hurt me. And I had to stop trying to expect myself to be perfect and then drinking to escape what I was instead. Now it's time for me to make amends."

Rob kept silent.

Within minutes the lake opened up in front of them and Rob could hear the squeals of children playing down by the water. The carefree happiness of being a young child at the lake flashed in his mind – running on the beach, his father making sand castles with him. He gazed at the picnic area with its wooden tables and barbecue pits and remembered the Ethans' lunches of fogged tumblers of cold drinks, sandwiches in tinfoil and seedy watermelon.

Next to the picnic area was the shadowy stand of trees he used to play in, where his mother would never follow. Now Rob understood why his mother had screamed at his father to chase after him in the woods – because she was terrified to go in.

Chapter 44

Mrs. Ethan wanted to drive Rob to the airport, so they stopped back at the Ethan house to pick up Rob's travel bags. As they drove up, Rob's dad was mounting a red flower box under the front window.

"Have a nice drive?" he asked, wiping his sweaty forehead.

"Wonderful," said Mrs. Ethan.

Rob went to his room and slung the straps of his big canvas duffle bag over his shoulders. When he came into the kitchen his father was holding his mother's hand across the table, though they let go soon as they saw him.

"Take care, buddy," his father said out on the front lawn, shaking Rob's hand. He gave his mom a peck on the cheek and said goodbye, returning to his nailing.

Rob and Mrs. Ethan walked together down the driveway "He's a good man," she said, brushing a loose strand of hair from her eyes. "I wonder what could have been if I'd been sober."

When they were in the car, she said, "Take a lesson from me, honey, learn to show your true feelings to people like your wife and close friends. I couldn't deal with mine and it got me in trouble, that's a good part of why I drank."

"I guess I'm not very good at talking about feelings, either."

"You'll have to try, like with your friend Alana. Do you feel like you're in love?"

"Yeah. I guess."

"Have you ever told her?"

"No."

"Why don't you?"

"Mother!" Rob looked out the window the rest of the way to Bud's house.

"Safe and sound," Mrs. Ethan pronounced, locking the door. "I sure didn't want to crash this baby up."

Moments later, Bud came around the side of the house, pulling off his soiled gardening gloves. He hugged them each warmly.

"So, young traveller, are you ready for the adventure of your life?"

"I'm only going to England for a week!" Rob protested.

"Surprises are always around the corner," said Bud confidently. "Sandra, you'll find Jeannie in the kitchen concocting some extravagant dish for supper. I'm going to bring my friend around to the garden for a chat."

They walked around to the back yard and sat down in large padded lawn chairs surrounded by a thicket of rosebushes.

"Alana must be dying to see you," Bud prompted.

"I don't know about that."

"Why not?"

"Sometimes I don't think I have that much to offer her."

"Oh? Why would that be?

Rob put his elbows on his knees. "I don't know," he sighed.

"Don't know too much about yourself, do you?" Bud asked.

"Maybe."

"Could that be because you cover up thoughts that might bother you?"

Rob stared into Bud's warm brown eyes. "I guess I try not to think about things that are crappy."

"You said a lot, Rob, about how you deal with problems – by

covering them up, looking away. Hiding problems is a way of trying to exert control over what you can't. It's like hiding your mother's booze."

"Well, if I try to control things, odds are better that crappy stuff won't happen," Rob said defensively.

"I find it's usually better to accept there's a problem, accept you feel bad and then let go for a while."

"How does that help?"

"You get to know yourself. Then you learn better what you can control and what you can't."

"How will I know the difference?" said Rob, losing patience.

"You have to have faith that your Higher Power will guide you to the answer."

Suddenly Rob connected with Bud's words. He felt a red dragon surface from his centre, float to the sky and lift the heaviness from his shoulders. He felt a moment of carefree joy.

"You OK?" Bud asked.

"That felt different for a second. I didn't know how it happened."

"No, Rob, that was perfectly normal. It's what happens when you let go. Now you have to learn how to make it last."

Chapter 45

The DC-8 would be landing in London in less than an hour. Then, finally, the nonstop hum of the plane's engines would end, thought Rob. He was exhausted, having been too uncomfortable to sleep on the overnight flight.

The blackness outside began to give way to an orange layer of light on the horizon ahead. This was the dawn of a new day quite different from any other of his life, he realized.

When he reached the gate, he looked around for Alana. There she was with an older woman in a large yellow hat whom he supposed was her mother.

Rob snaked through the large crowd in Alana's direction.

"Hi, stranger," she said, wrapping her arms around him. He took the hug stiffly, nervous under the benevolent eye of Mrs. Stewart.

"You're in for glorious weather, Rob," Mrs. Stewart remarked. She was blond and sunny-faced like Alana.

"Mummy, he came to see me, not the silly weather," Alana retorted, squeezing Rob's arm.

They drove to Bath, where Alana's family had lived and where they were now renting a house from another professor who was on sabbatical. Driving on the wrong side of the highway put Rob slightly on edge at first. But then he relaxed and gazed curiously at the long, tightly packed rows of houses with laundry hanging in their yards.

Rob and Alana sat on a stiff antique couch in the living room.

"So Rob, what would you like to see first? I'm your personal tour guide. It's a very old town, you realize, known primarily for its Roman baths and Georgian architecture. In the eighteenth century, Bath became England's premier spa, where the rich and famous came to take the waters. At that time the architect John Wood designed many of the honey-coloured Georgian stone buildings that give Bath its distinctive appearance."

"Alana, I think I need to catch a nap first. I didn't sleep very well on the plane."

"Fine. Nap today, tour tomorrow. But how about meeting some of my old girlfriends at the Beehive tonight? I told them how cute you are and they really want to meet you."

"Sounds fine. But first I need to sack out or the bags under my eyes will ruin my good looks."

"Right! I'll show you to your room."

"I don't get to sleep with you?" teased Rob.

"We've already had that discussion." Alana leaned over and kissed Rob. He returned her kiss swiftly, uncomfortable with the thought of parents in the next room.

Rob dumped his bag and closed the blinds, then threw himself onto the quilt-covered bed. At first he tossed and turned as though still on the plane, but then a deep sleep came. When he awoke, it felt much later in the day.

He found a note on the kitchen table from Alana saying they'd gone to pick up groceries. He helped himself to an apple from a fruit bowl on the counter and ambled out into a small grassy yard edged with tall blooming tulips.

What a place for practising his *Seisan kata!* He practised block and punch combinations till he felt loose, then he worked on his kicking drills. Rob tried to feel rooted to the ground but at the same time pliable enough to allow for free movement. No thoughts, no mind, he counselled himself, yet total awareness and focus.

He bowed to the east and brought his arms up in *Sanchin* position with finger tips to the sky. Then he executed three *Sanchin* arm thrusts and a circular strike where both hands were meant to land on the temples of the attacker.

Following three circular palm-heel strikes to the face, Rob dropped both of his hands with the right hand sitting on the left pointing up like a knife and then thrust them up together and sliced the throat of his imaginary attacker.

Further on, he blocked an imaginary club attack, then drove the point of his elbow into his attacker's sternum. Wheeling to face a second attacker, he brought his fisted right hand up high and down to the side of the assailant's head in a hammer strike.

"Don't kill anyone!" Alana was watching from inside the back door.

"How long were you standing there?"

"Long enough to see how deadly you are!" she laughed. "Come in for supper, killer."

Chapter 46

As Alana scanned the Beehive Pub for her friends Sara and Jane, she explained to Rob that they had gone to public school with Alana and were now at the University of Bath. Jane turned out to be a thin, tall brunette and Sara had rosy freckled cheeks.

"Hello, Rob, delighted to meet you," said Sara.

"Pleasure," said Jane. "Alana told us you were a black belt. Fancy that!"

"Heavens, Jane! I said *almost* a black belt," Alana corrected.

"In any event, I'm sure there's no one tougher than you around here," said Sara with a cheery smile.

"Sara, don't encourage him!" Alana joked.

Rob basked in the attention, never having hung out with three girls who all appeared to like him. He could get used to this, he decided. What fun, as these girls might express it.

Within a minute, however, two other guys stopped by their booth. Sara made a sour face and said hello, and Alana ignored them. After they had moved off and seated themselves two booths down, Rob asked, "Who are they?"

"Creeps. Especially the smaller one."

"An old boyfriend?" Rob asked cautiously.

"He wishes," said Jane. "He put the moves on Alana a few weeks ago."

"I'll say! He even got a tad rough," added Sara.

"What do you mean, rough?" asked Rob, heating up.

"Drop it, Rob!" Alana said, sipping her beer.

"No." Rob's voice escalated. "I want to know what he did to you."

"He tried to make out with me on the way home from here one night, and wouldn't take no for an answer."

"Did he –?" Rob fumed.

"Don't be ridiculous! I used some of those moves you taught me."

"She certainly put Billy in his place," Sara added.

"Now I'll put him in his place," Rob muttered, slamming his glass down on the table.

"Now Rob, kindly don't make a scene," Alana scolded.

But for the rest of his beer he only half-listened to the chatter as his mind raced with what he'd like to do to that Billy.

At 10:30, Sara and Jane prepared to leave. They both had summer jobs to go to in the morning.

Alana looked at her watch. "We should probably leave as well, Rob, so we'll rise early for the grand tour."

As she walked her friends to the door, however, Rob sauntered over to Billy's table.

Billy glanced up. "Hi, mate. What's up?"

"Bother her again and you're dead meat, man."

"Whoa! Look at the tough bloke coming over to court our girls. Why don't you piss off, mate?"

"I'm warning you. Don't mess with her," Rob said, as pub patrons turned to stare.

"Rob, leave him alone," Alana barked from the doorway. "Let's go." She went outside with her friends.

Rob left Billy's table, muttering coarsely under his breath, and strode quickly to catch up to the girls. "Alana, wait, I'm sorry."

She kept walking, and Rob took her hand. "I gave him a little warning, that's all."

"I told you not to start anything, you didn't listen to me."

A loud voice came from behind them. "Hey, mate, I want a word with you."

Billy and his companion were catching up to them, followed by a gang of teenagers. Rob let go of Alana's hand and took a sparring stance, raising his hands so he'd be ready to deflect an attack.

"Oh my, its Mr. Kung-Fu himself," laughed Billy.

Rob felt the urge to turn and run and heard himself breathing hard. Control the breath, he thought. Find the dragon breath.

When Billy ran towards him Rob reacted without thought. His left arm whipped in a blocking circle and caught Billy's right hook in mid-flight. Then the protruding lower knuckles of Rob's fist shot up and curved towards Billy's head and struck him hard in the temple. Billy's legs buckled.

"Rob, stop!" shouted Alana.

He grabbed Billy's right hand and executed a wrist lock by bending his palm back towards his chest and then snapping it in a twisting motion to the side. Billy went limp and dropped to his knees, his face contorted.

Just as Rob heard Alana holler "Oh my God!" he felt a blow from behind crash into his ribs. He dropped Billy's hand, his ribs exploding in pain. He turned to face this new threat from the rear, wheezing to breathe, in time to see Billy's friend just miss a second kick with his steel-toed boot.

"Stop, everyone!" Rob heard Alana scream. But he had no choice now, he had to face his second attacker. The guy raised his fists in a boxing stance, and Rob caught his eyes and glared as he shuffled in closer. The teenagers jeered and yelled.

The guy's right jab missed his nose by a few inches. Then he threw a left jab, which Rob blocked, then hooked his leg around and struck the guy's ribs. He screwed his other foot into the ground and rotated his hips into the kick to give it as much power as he could muster.

When he saw the guy's arm press against his ribs he knew his attacker was in pain. "Kill him, for Chrissakes!" Billy yelled at his friend. The guy lunged forward to grab Rob's shirt. When Rob felt fingernails sinking into his chest, he shot up his hands like a knife to break the hold and buried his knee in his attacker's ribs.

The second attacker tried another jab at Rob, but Rob blocked it and countered with a hard *shoken* knuckle strike to his attacker's lower rib cage. Rob dug his raised knuckle into the skin, spreading the flesh between his ribs. Then Rob deflected another jab to his face and countered with an open left hand, striking his attacker in the nose with the heel of his palm.

Rob felt something collapse in the other boy's face, and thought, he's done. His assailant stumbled back, his hands clasping his nose, a trail of red following him on the pavement. Then Rob turned to Billy, who'd been egging his friend on.

He stood in a fighting stance with hands up and open, thinking of Sensei's expression "glaring eyes, fast hands." The spirit of the dragon filled Rob when his eyes met Billy's. His hands rotated in a blur, performing two circle blocks to deflect any attack.

Nothing else moved. Then Billy stuttered, "Forget it, mate. The fight's over."

Rob turned to Alana, who was crying.

"It's all right," he reassured her, holding her arms. "I had no choice, the guy jumped me."

Chapter 47

Rob kept his arm around Alana as they pressed on home. She was still shaking and crying when they reached the Stewart residence.

Alana's parents had been watching television, but turned their attention when they saw Alana and Rob.

"We had a little trouble at the restaurant." Rob spoke up immediately to counteract any impression that they had been fighting between themselves.

"What kind of trouble?" Mr. Stewart demanded.

Alana wiped her eyes. "Rob got into an argument with some bloke who'd been bothering me a few weeks back. Then when we left the pub, this bloke and his mate followed Rob out to beat him up."

"Are you all right, Rob?" asked Alana's mother, scanning Rob's face for injury, but not seeing any.

"Yes, ma'am. I handled it."

"It was two against one," Alana sniffled.

"Hardly sporting," the professor said. "But you look like you acquitted yourself rather well."

"Rob's a black belt," Alana blurted.

"Not quite yet," Rob explained.

"Anyway, he sent them running off with their tails between their legs. I think he broke one fellow's nose."

"Sorry to drag your daughter into this, sir. But the guy was a jerk to her and I had to let him know he couldn't get away with it."

"I see that chivalry is alive and well in 1976. It appears you have acquired a knight in shining armour, Alana."

"I believe I can take care of myself, thank you!"

"Certainly, my dear, that's how we raised you. Right, then." The professor and Mrs. Stewart returned to their program.

Rob and Alana went into the den and collapsed together on a brown leather coach.

"I'm sorry about picking the fight, Alana. In the past, I would have walked away, but I've never been that angry before. I wanted to kill that guy."

"So, you do get mad after all. Welcome to the human race," she said sternly. "That doesn't mean you have to go put yourself in the guy's face."

"I didn't even feel I had a choice. I don't know what happened to me."

"Look, all that's happening is you've likely stomped down your emotions for so long you don't know what to do when they pop up."

"I guess," Rob said confusedly.

"When you feel angry, acknowledge you're angry and accept it. You don't have to numb your feelings out, but you don't necessarily have to act on them either."

"So I shouldn't go around beating up people?" Rob poked Alana and made her smile.

"No, you big bully. But I don't think you have to worry; no one is going to challenge you around here."

"I'll be gone soon in any case." His smile vanished. "Look, I've been thinking, maybe I shouldn't tour around London on my own the day before I fly back. Why don't you come with me?"

"My parents wouldn't permit it."

"Then I'll stay here with you."

"No, Rob, you should see London before you go home, you may never get back. Besides, I'll tell you what to see and where to stay."

Rob looked away, but he couldn't keep his face expressionless.

"You look so sad. Tell me what you're feeling," Alana said sympathetically.

"You know how I feel."

"You've alluded to it, but I've never heard you say anything directly."

"Alana, this is like the Spanish Inquisition."

"This is something you have to work on, Rob."

"Fine. I'm sad about leaving you at the end of the week. I'll really miss you."

"Good, that's something. Let's hear the rest. How do you feel about *me?*" Alana pushed.

Rob's face reddened. "This is weird," he muttered.

"I'm waiting. You've got ten seconds to say something direct or you can fly home right now."

"Al*right!* Alana, I fell for you the moment I first saw you. I've thought about you night and day."

"Really!" she giggled.

"Yes, really. Now it's your turn. How do you feel about me?"

"I have to admit I didn't pay much attention to you at first," Alana said. "But that changed."

"Oh yes? How?"

"Now you're giving me the Inquisition!"

"That's right, Alana. It's your turn to feel the heat."

"Fine. At first I thought you were a tad strange. Don't give me that hurt look! You didn't say much and you just stared at me in class."

"That was shyness," Rob said defensively.

“I understand now.”

“So what changed?”

“I realized you’re a pretty bright guy who is seriously cute!”

“That’s better.”

“But there was always something sad about you.”

“Oh, God. Don’t say you felt sorry for me, it would kill me.”

“I didn’t. But it was a challenge for me to find out what kind of person you were, beyond the silent macho karate type that never says much. Deep down, I found out, you were a sweet guy. And you’ve got a sexy butt too!”

“Yours ain’t bad, either.”

“So don’t get serious with anyone else before I come back,” she warned Rob.

“Well, don’t you, either.”

She closed her eyes and leaned forward, and Rob met her lips with his.

“Alana.”

“Yes?”

“I feel maybe things are starting to change. I mean maybe there is hope after all.”

“Hope for what?” Alana ran her hand through his hair.

“For me. That I might be happy someday.”

“You aren’t happy right now?” Alana said, frowning.

“Of course I am. But I mean happy about my life in general. Mostly I’ve just existed.”

“Well, that makes sense. You’ve had a difficult upbringing. But sooner or later you’re going to wake up and realize that you’re in charge. You get to live your life the way you like.”

“I think I realize that. Everything feels really different now.”

“Different from when?”

Rob stumbled with words that didn’t want to come out. “From

before Julius died."

"Look, that was a horrible tragedy for you, Rob. Yet I'll bet you've never even cried about it."

"I never cry," Rob said, feeling flushed as though he were getting ill.

"Fine. You've had a difficult life, and now Julius was your best friend and he killed himself. You have a lot to cry about."

The familiar pain in Rob's stomach and chest flared up. It moved higher into his chest. Then it travelled up his throat and face to his eyes. His body shook, and Alana sat there and held Rob. She put a tissue to one of his eyes and then the other.

Suddenly he felt a strong feeling of trust. He wanted to put it into words, but all he could say was, "I love you, Alana."

"I love you too, Rob.

"Do you mind if I kiss you?"

"Of course not."

He kissed her and touched her breast.

"My parents are out there," she warned.

"Sorry."

"No, that's alright. I'll lock the door."

Chapter 48

On the departure platform they kissed and hugged until it was time for Rob to board the train.

"I'll see you in the fall and we'll resume where we left off," she said.

"Love you," he said again, marvelling as the words left his lips.

Alana's face shone. "Me too. Keep well, my love."

Rob climbed up the stairs to the train car and took one of the blue polyester seats. Alana waved and smiled from the platform as long as he could see her. A surge of loneliness filled him, but he tried to savour the sensation and feel alive. He imagined that his first eighteen years were flying past him so now he could begin life again.

After a while, he picked up his London travel guide and scanned the advertisements for bed and breakfasts, as the Stewarts had recommended. Geez, there are so many and some are way too expensive, he thought.

"Are you travelling to London?" asked a well-modulated voice. It came from the young man across the aisle. He was wearing a foreign-looking blue print shirt and had deep brown skin, a thin nose and gentle dark eyes.

"Yes, for one night. My flight home leaves tomorrow evening."

The young man crossed the aisle and sat down next to Rob.

"Where do you come from?"

"Canada. How about you?"

"India, but I study at Bath University. I am also going home for a vacation and spending a day in London. I have cousins in Toronto, maybe you know them?"

"I doubt it. Toronto's a pretty big city."

"Yes, but big is a relative concept," he said smiling. "My name is Anil."

"I'm Rob." They shook hands. "What city are you from in India?

"Shimla. It's the capital of Himachal Pradesh, in the northern region of India. Very pretty with snow-capped peaks."

"I thought India was hot."

"It is in the south. Shimla was a summer retreat of the imperial British, who went there to escape the heat."

"Cool."

"Yes, it is nice and cool there. We have many English-style shops and even ice cream parlours. I was most anxious to study in England after my upper-level schooling was completed."

"I'm not sure my own city is that exotic," Rob said sheepishly.

"No? But I have observed that North Americans are very wealthy. Everyone there drives big cars."

"That's partly true," said Rob. "But not students like me. We take the bus."

"So you are a student as well! What are you studying?"

"Philosophy and some other stuff."

"Ah yes, Mr. Russell and Mr. Hume. I have read their works. May I inquire where you are staying in London?" Anil asked.

"Well, I was looking at this travel guide to find a place."

"We find ourselves in similar circumstances, I believe. Perhaps it would be cheaper if we find a place with double accommodation?"

"Sure. We can hang together," Rob said.

"That would be most acceptable as long as there is no rope involved."

Chapter 49

Rob and Anil descended from the train with knapsacks on their backs and manoeuvred through a sea of languages and nationalities. At the exit doors of Victoria Station they checked Rob's map. There was a cluster of bed and breakfasts east of the station so they set out in that direction.

Rob's mood was sombre – each step he took from the train station was one step further from Alana. What if her interest in him faded while they were apart? Out of sight, out of mind – wasn't that the expression? Meanwhile, the morning was warm and Rob's brow was perspiring. He stopped to take off his coat and hike his duffle bag back onto his shoulder.

Anil was coping better with the heat in his sandals and light cottons. He walked slowly, and each of his steps seemed deliberate and measured. Rob found he had to match Anil's pace with half-steps in order to not get ahead of him.

They approached a street of bed and breakfasts, and when Rob looked in the guide he noted that the first one's rates were within his budget if it was shared between two.

"Let's check this place out. My friend Alana told me I should look at the room before paying."

"Most certainly. Is your friend from London?"

"No, but she's English. But her family just moved to Canada this year, so she's back in England for the summer. I just left her to go back to Canada. We had quite a thing going."

"I am certain that you feel as though someone has given you a hard blow to the midsection."

Rob smiled, knowing the exact feeling from sparring in karate. "Almost that bad, but not quite."

The lobby was decorated with garish red wallpaper. A stocky, grizzled man sat behind the counter reading a newspaper and barely looked up when the two young men entered.

"Excuse me, I wondered if you could show us a room?" Rob asked.

"Right-o," said the proprietor, obviously annoyed at being asked to get up.

He walked them to the third floor, unlocked a door and threw the room open to them. It was buzzing with flies.

Rob turned to the proprietor. "I'm not sure we can deal with the flies."

"No problem, mate. I'll be right back."

As they waited for the proprietor to return, Rob said to Anil, "I don't think this is the place for us." Anil nodded vigorously in agreement.

The proprietor reappeared with a can of bug spray, which he obviously relished shooting in every direction. "No flies now," he pronounced.

"Uh, I think we'll keep looking," said Rob.

Outside, Anil said, "That man has much to learn about inn-keeping. It was most disagreeable for him to kill with no purpose."

After passing on a few more seedy establishments, they arrived in front of Mrs. Grimes' Guest Bed and Breakfast. Here there were neat white flower boxes and a large red mat that announced, Welcome.

Mrs. Grimes was a large woman with red cheeks and blue-rinsed hair. She greeted the travellers warmly. "Scorcher of a day, loves. I'll fix you up with a room at the back; it's a tad cooler there. Take this key and have a tiny peek, would you? And let me know if it's to your liking."

They walked up a flight of wooden stairs to the second floor and found a small room with a bed on each side. They were old military-style iron bed frames with thin mattresses, but at least the linen seemed clean. On the mirror was a hand-written sign, No Girls in The Rooms, Except Marrieds.

"Let's take it, OK?" suggested Rob hopefully. He was exhausted from the search.

"I agree. This room is humble but agreeable."

Hot and sweaty, Rob proceeded to the showers. After stripping down, he had no luck getting hot water from the hot water tap. Eventually he realized that he had to insert coins in a meter for hot water. But since he had none with him, he peeled off his underwear and danced in the frigid spray.

When he returned to the room, Anil was sitting on the bed in lotus fashion.

"The heat not bothering you, eh?" said Rob, admiringly.

"Heat is a relative term," Anil said enigmatically. "After all, it is necessary for it to be hot sometimes for cold to exist, and vice versa."

Rob thought of the air conditioner in his father's bedroom that blasted cold air on hot summer days. He decided it was a less elegant solution than Anil's method of attitude adjustment.

After their rest Rob found himself hungry and suggested they set out for Piccadilly Circus to find a restaurant, as Alana had recommended.

Lord Nelson in the distance began to tower over them as they approached Trafalgar Square. Rob and Anil stopped to gaze up at the impressive sculpture perched on the spiralling column.

Fifty paces away was a statue of a lion as large as a Buick; a teenager had climbed on it and was pretending to ride it. "That fellow is very likely from Texas, wouldn't you agree?" Anil proposed.

"Quite possibly!" Rob laughed. He was glad that he had made a friend to see London with. It made the first day away from Alana more bearable.

They found a fish-and-chips shop, though Anil ordered his chips with a salad. As they slurped on lemonade they talked about the subjects they had studied.

"We studied one Canadian author in our literature class," Anil announced. "Robertson Davies. I liked his book very much, I thought it was very insightful. The task of the lead character was to learn that he was not meant to be the lead character, but the fifth. That is what we believe in India – that everybody must try to accept their place in life."

"I don't think people believe that in North America," said Rob. "Everybody is striving to be number one, and if they aren't they're disappointed." He thought of how he had felt when he had come in second in the karate tournament.

When their food arrived, Rob looked for the ketchup. He was about to ask for some when he realized the vinegar on the table was for chips. He reached too quickly for it and knocked his water glass over, soaking himself and Anil.

"I'm so sorry," he muttered. It was like him to make a bad impression on a new friend.

Anil took some paper napkins and helped Rob mop up the table. "You must practice mindfulness, my friend," he said with a grin.

"I have to practice being less clumsy, that's for sure."

"Being less clumsy comes from mindfulness, I assure you. I have noticed that you are always in a hurry. You walk quickly to your destination and then you wish to settle things as soon as possible. You are always trying to get to the future and do not dwell very much in the present."

Rob felt the urge to defend his character, but he said nothing, sensing no unkindness in Anil's voice.

"What were you thinking of when you knocked over the water glass?" Anil asked him.

Rob thought for a moment, "Well, I was hungry and was thinking how I wanted to taste the french fries. Isn't that living in the present?"

"Not quite, my friend. When you reached for the vinegar cruet you were focused on satisfying your hunger. If instead you had looked at the bottle and focused on picking it up and sprinkling your fries in a controlled fashion, you would not have knocked over your water."

"But it's impossible to focus on your motions all day long. You can't think every time you move."

"Some masters do."

"How do they learn to do that?"

"Through meditation. In meditation one teaches the mind to be present by recognizing each thought. Thus, instead of the mind being a train without a conductor that takes you places you do not wish to go, you can become the conductor and direct the train to the destination you seek."

Rob liked the idea of being more in control of his mind. "But how do you learn to do that?"

"As you are meditating, you practice acknowledging each thought that enters your mind. Afterwards you are able to more easily disregard the chatter in your mind and concentrate on a task at hand without distraction. If you must wash the floor with a mop, you think with great interest about mopping the floor efficiently."

"Huh. When I'm doing menial jobs I take my mind off them by thinking about other stuff."

"Like what?"

"Like all the school work I have got to get done."

"You mean, you worry."

"Yes, I worry and get stressed out."

"For what reason?"

"I'm not sure. I worry about whether I am smart enough to do my assignments and get a good mark. It's kind of like a tape recorder in my mind playing the same old thing over and over."

"You must learn to notice when the tape recorder is playing in your mind and turn it off. It is not healthy to constantly repeat negative ideas. If you continue to tell yourself that you will not accomplish things, then over time you and others will adhere to that opinion."

"You have a point," granted Rob.

Rob took a mouthful of haddock, enjoying the freshness and the light batter.

"This is great fish, Anil. Do you want to try some?"

"Thank you, I don't eat fish. But it seems you are learning already."

"What do you mean?"

"Your mind is focused on the taste of the fish, rather than being a million miles away. You should try to practice this habit in all of your daily activities. Every time you get a negative thought or worry, recognize that it is merely a thought, then demand that your mind think about the task at hand – or in this case, the fish."

Rob concentrated on chewing the fish and chips and experiencing how they tasted.

"If you focus on enjoying the present and keeping your mind under control, you will have great happiness," Anil prophesied.

A piece of apple pie would be great for dessert, Rob suddenly thought. But then he observed that he would have to wait until it was in front of him before he could savour it. So he decided he might as well stick to the fish and chips for the moment.

Chapter 50

Now that they had a room and had eaten, Rob lay on his bed, wrestling with indecision about what to do with the rest of the day. There was so much to see in London in so little time.

"What should we do this afternoon? Check out Big Ben? The Tower of London?"

"I would recommend that we visit St. Paul's Cathedral to investigate Christopher Wren's famous architectural design."

"Cool."

So they went out to Victoria Street to catch a bus. The one that arrived was double-decker, and they scampered up the staircase so they could observe the street scenery on the way to the cathedral.

Rob found it neat to watch the fashionably modern people walking alongside buildings that were hundreds of years old. The gargoyles on the sides of the old buildings seemed to be staring out at the crowds, warding off the new era with their eyes.

Seeing all of the interesting buildings and people from the slow-moving bus, Rob again became aware of everything he was missing and anxious that they wouldn't make the most of their time in London. "I hope St. Paul's is open," he remarked, wishing they had checked the hours in the tourist guide.

Anil smiled and said, "I don't hope that it is or that it isn't."

"But we're wasting our time if we can't even go in."

"You would be disappointed if it is closed?"

"Of course!"

"Then why do you hope it is open?"

"You've lost me, Anil."

"If you would be disappointed to find the cathedral closed, then you should not hope it will be open," Anil explained, "for then you are setting yourself up to be upset, if reality does not conform to your desires."

"Anil, that's crazy. Are you saying we should never hope for things to turn out a certain way?"

Anil paused and looked out the window and searched for where they were on the street and then looked down at his street map.

"Yes, Rob. That is what I am saying. Most of us go through life living for the future – that is what hope is. We are hoping our life will become better and our suffering will end, when the truth is that our desires are what causes our suffering. Every time we like this or hate that, or hope to attain this or avoid that, we walk over a bed of coals."

"Don't they walk on coals for real in India? Have you done it?"

Anil chuckled. "I am not a fire-walker, although I have seen it done by my cousin Sanji. I assure you that walking on a bed of fiery coals would change your attitude towards fear and danger."

Rob was intrigued but also scared by the idea. "But doesn't fear protect you from doing stupid things?"

"Yes, but it holds you in a frozen state. Fear is like hope – it anticipates the future without evidence. Instead of fearing, we should consult the evidence as to whether the action we are contemplating will prove harmful."

"But we could burn our feet, for God's sake!"

"If you have witnessed others walking on the coals without

injury, what is the objective basis for fear? The right course of action is to stop reacting to everything that happens around you. You know – I am afraid of this and that. Instead, look at what is happening before you and see that your fear is empty, that it is based on past experiences that feel like they are happening right now, but are not. You move beyond fear by acknowledging its presence."

"You can't deny that bad things happen to people, Anil."

"I agree that life is difficult and painful at times. Indeed, acceptance of the difficulties of life is the first step to freeing ourselves from suffering. If I accept that tomorrow will not always be better it will aid me to focus on the here and now. We must vow that we will surrender to whatever happens that is difficult, and that we won't run away or fight, but rather accept and ask what our choices are, and pick the one that is in keeping with who we are."

Finally Anil caught a glimpse of St. Paul's Cathedral ahead and pulled the bus-cord, and he and Rob descended from the bus and crossed the street. They went up to read the hours posted by the door.

"It looks like it's open after all," Rob said sheepishly.

"See? You did not have to worry," said Anil, and gave a little bow.

Then they walked through the cathedral doors and gazed up at the great dome, awestruck by the majestic grandeur of the rising space.

On the way back to Mrs. Grimes', Rob was solemn. The beauty of the cathedral had brought up his feelings. His sadness was double – he had just left the girl he loved and the next day, he realized, he would leave a new friend as well. He hoped they would keep in touch.

"What are your plans for the summer, Anil?"

"I am going to work with Sri Rama Mata, a holy man and a friend of our family. He runs the Calcutta Homeless Shelter."

"That sounds inspiring," said Rob. "Do you work there to earn money?"

"Not exactly, rather I do so to emulate his spirit. Sri Rama Mata is a large man with big hands. He literally picks up the unfortunates in the street who are near death and carries them in his arms to the shelter. There he bathes and feeds them and nurses them as best he can, though some of the poor souls are sadly so diseased and malnourished that they die within days. I would like to model my life after Sri Rama Mata."

Rob listened intently, sensing that Anil was sharing something vitally important to him.

"I have listened to Sri Rama Mata speak about the children of the street who have died in his arms. He feels sad, yet he does not become anxious or upset, but remains serene. He strokes their small heads so tenderly that they meet death without fear."

A chill of loneliness made Rob shudder. "Anil, it seems kinda scary to do this work. How can you not be afraid of people dying around you?"

"I do not know the answer to that question yet. But Sri Rama Mata says we should think of fear as a wall in front of where we wish to go. We should put a hand and then a foot on top of the wall. When we are on top, we can jump down on the other side. Then we will act not out of fear, but from a tender heart and out of compassion for others. It is wonderful to watch Sri Rama Mata working in the shelter. He seems so full of energy, so youthful, and he stays so positive and cheery in the most trying circumstances and difficult cases."

"Sri Rama Mata sounds like a very impressive man. Wow," said Rob.

"Yes, but the odd thing is that he remains very modest. He

does not say 'I am wonderful, am I not?' He does not count the lives he has saved. He is humble and gentle and opens his heart fully to anyone who comes to speak to him or who needs help."

"How does he do that?" asked Rob, thinking about his own tendency to be closed to people.

"He believes it is his duty to enlighten all sentient beings on this earth, and that the first step is to recognize the essential goodness of everything."

"Can anybody do that? I mean, recognize that everything is good?" Rob asked.

"I believe we can. When we were in St. Paul's Cathedral, we stood beneath the dome and simply experienced the joy of being there, not trying to think or understand but just being in that space. It seemed perfect. We were alive, just experiencing the reality of such grandeur. Sri Rama Mata believes that all life on earth and the beauty of our world is basically good. You have to take this belief in goodness and include your own self in this golden light."

"OK. But do you mind if we start by embracing the goodness of the wicked-looking chocolates in that store's window?"

After dinner, they wandered slowly back to Mrs. Grimes' to hang out in their narrow room until bedtime. Anil sat cross-legged on his bed and Rob lay with his head in his hands, trying to embrace the goodness of the large spider lurking on the cracked ceiling over his pillow.

It was silly to worry about the spider, he told himself. But he couldn't completely keep his mind from returning to the image of it crawling across his face in the middle of the night.

"Anil," Rob finally asked, "how did you learn to control your mind?"

"In our family, my siblings and I grew up with the concepts of mindfulness and Buddhist values. Sri Rama Mata often spoke to us about these."

"What are they?"

"Sri Rama Mata taught us that there are six virtues on the path to enlightenment. The first is generosity. You should never expect reward or acknowledgment of your deeds or ever regret your act of generosity. Giving should be done out of happiness and pleasure. I believe there is great freedom when one eliminates the craving for more things."

Rob thought about Bud. "I know someone who's rich but enjoys giving stuff away, since he learnt that more money does not make him any happier."

"Ah! Your friend is a *bodhisattva.*"

"A what?"

"A *bodhisattva.* A person who realizes that to give away possessions and attainments for the benefit of others is the path of freedom."

"Bod-hi-satt-va. I'll have to tell him that," Rob smiled.

"The next virtue is ethics, not doing that which could be harmful to others. Although, we have to be careful not to be ethical to impress others, but rather for its own sake."

"I got you there," said Rob, as he flipped over and propped his chin on his hands, looking at Anil. "Nothing bugs me more than when people act good because they think you're watching."

"Ah, Rob. You must be careful, because the third virtue is patience. When someone's behaviour causes you to become angry, then your mind loses its calmness and reasoning ability. To be patient you need to see that the person annoying you is himself experiencing negative emotions, therefore there is no point in becoming angry. So, next time someone does something that would upset you, thank him for allowing you to test your patience and to practice peace of mind."

"Yeah, right!"

"Do not laugh! I believe you already try to do this."

"I do?"

"Yes, in your martial arts, where you must be able to receive pain without losing your judgment. This is where courage is sometimes very important. If a warrior is struck by his opponent's sword and begins to bleed, he must not lose his determination and give up. Rather, he must rally himself and fight with all his strength, power and courage. That is the true character of a warrior."

It was true, Rob thought. Sensei had taught him that the moment he felt afraid or angry about being hurt he'd lost the fight. Sensei said that it was necessary to lose one's ego, that it was not about looking good for the crowd. Yet when Rob was hit, he would be embarrassed and lose his concentration on his strength and power. Rob dwelled on Anil's point of thanking his opponent for hitting him. This was what Sensei must have meant – that by taking ego and self out of the picture, the mind, body and spirit could fuse naturally into one.

Anil was continuing. "The fourth virtue is constant effort, which is needed to overcome laziness – including that kind of laziness known as lack of confidence."

"Why is that laziness?" asked Rob, stung, since lack of confidence was what everyone accused him of.

"I will explain. The first time you have to do a task, you may try to avoid it by telling yourself you cannot accomplish it, correct?"

"I guess."

"But after you have once completed the task and you have to repeat it, it is much easier, is it not? That means that by exerting effort, most goals are attainable. Since it is only the lack of confidence that impedes you from exerting yourself, it is a kind of laziness, is it not?"

"Maybe."

"In order to exert constant effort you also need concentration, which is the fifth virtue."

"That's something you already told me I had to work on, when I knocked over the water," Rob said sulkily.

"Don't take my criticisms personally, Rob. Most people's minds are distracted by the world and thus fail to concentrate fully. But if you can learn to concentrate your mind, you can accomplish nearly any goal through appropriate effort."

"So what is the sixth virtue?" said Rob, feeling like he might as well get all the bad news about himself at once.

"All of these deeds are led by wisdom. In order to find enlightenment it is one's wisdom that shows the way to the end … but let's continue this discussion another time," said Anil, whose eyes were starting to droop.

Rob suddenly realized that he, too, was exhausted by all of this information. When he turned out the light he fell asleep almost immediately.

Chapter 51

In the morning Rob was wakened by a sharp beam of light in the crack between the green canvas drapes. He turned to see if Anil was also awake. But Anil's bed was empty, and Rob's heart leaped at the fear that his friend had left him.

Then he noticed Anil on the floor by the sink, sitting in a lotus position with his back erect and his hands palm up and relaxed on his knees.

Rob quietly tiptoed into the hall with his towel and clothes, this time with change for the hot water meter in his pants pocket. Bearing in mind what Anil had taught him yesterday, he tried to slow his pace, concentrating on the motions of his fingers washing his hair and the feeling of the towel drying each part of his body.

When he returned to the room, he turned the doorknob slowly and peeked in to see if Anil was still meditating. Instead, his friend was lying on his bed looking at the map.

"Good morning, Rob."

Rob sat down on his own bed. "Do you sit like that every morning?"

"Yes. I try to meditate as long as I can stay calm. Today it wasn't that long!"

"Oh, sorry I interrupted you," said Rob.

"You did not. I am so excited about going to the British Museum today that I found myself fighting the urge to hurry and go. That is when I most need to meditate!"

"If you want two things at once, to go and to stay, can meditation even make your mind stop fighting with itself?"

"Over time it can, by helping you realize that wanting to hurry and wanting to stay are just thoughts and not reality. The mind can be very superficial and repetitive – it says what it is programmed to say, over and over again."

"Don't I know it!" said Rob. "I have a lot of thoughts that bug me and I'd love to find a way to turn them off."

"You can't turn off thoughts," warned Anil. "They are very mischievous and are strengthened by attempts to get rid of them. But if you learn how to notice thoughts, accept them and then let them go, they will eventually run out of energy and dissolve."

"How do I do that?" said Rob, desperate to know.

"Try this," said Anil. "Every time a negative thought appears, imagine you are writing it down on a piece of paper and tossing into a fire. If it reappears, write it down and throw it into the fire again. If you keep doing this over and over, eventually the thought will notice that you aren't accepting it, and it will dissolve."

"That doesn't sound too hard," said Rob. "I'll try it."

"Excellent!" said Anil. "My first pupil, I wish you great success. Would you like to go to breakfast now?"

"Yeah, I'm starved," said Rob. Then he felt embarrassed, remembering that Anil would shortly be helping people who were genuinely starving.

They proceeded downstairs to the dining area and through the doorway to the kitchen. They saw Mrs. Grimes at the stove. The enticing smell of bacon and sausages floated towards them. "You boys hungry?" she bellowed, wiping her hands on her smock.

"Yes ma'am!" Rob called out.

Mrs. Grimes brought a platter of scrambled eggs and bacon

and sausage links to the table.

"No, thank you very much," said Anil, lifting his hand as Mrs. Grimes offered him some. He had already helped himself to a banana and an apple and a few slices of bread.

She served Rob's plate and he began immediately to eat. The bacon was cooked almost black and it crumbled deliciously as soon as Rob put it in his mouth.

"Why don't you eat meat, Anil?" said Rob, not able to imagine giving up bacon.

"I don't believe in killing higher life forms to survive when we can eat lower ones."

"Like vegetables?"

"Exactly. Although, perhaps they feel pain as well when we kill them. How are we to know?"

Rob thought of a pig crying out in pain as it was butchered, and his appetite waned. Then he thought of an apple crying out as it was being bitten. That just seemed silly.

The British Museum was a huge stone building with dozens of pigeon-covered steps leading up to it. When they entered its tall doors and looked at the map of the museum, Rob realized it would actually take a week to see the displays of all of the great cultures and that they would have to focus on a few exhibits.

"I want to see the mummies," said Rob, always having been fascinated by the Egyptian pyramids.

"As for me, I am interested in seeing the famous Elgin marbles immortalized in Keats' poem," said Anil.

Each gallery they wandered through was a testimony to the rich legacy of human history on the planet. The Greek marble horses that Anil had wanted to see were extremely beautiful, catching the energy of the living horses in stone for all eternity.

"The sculptures explain why I do not eat meat," said Anil. "They reveal the eternal spirit of these animals, which we have no right to tamper with."

The Egyptian exhibit showed how the ancient Egyptians honoured the spirits of their dead relatives and leaders as well as their living, even to the point burying riches in their tombs.

"I guess they're kind of *bodhisattvas* themselves," joked Rob.

"In a manner of speaking," said Anil.

Rob was excited to see all the famous creations, but at the same time he felt sad, sensing a spirit of beauty in them that did not seem to exist in his own time.

"Anil, what has happened to people in the twentieth century?" Rob wondered.

"We have left the world of art for speed and technology." Anil replied. "Nowadays, people are concerned only with racing through life, not with stopping to cherish the wonders on this earth."

As they walked towards Mrs. Grimes' Rob thought about how different Anil was from any other person Rob knew. He felt touched by the fleeting contact with this young man.

When they got to the bed and breakfast, Rob fished through his pocket for change. "I want to use the pay phone here and give Alana a call before I leave."

"Do you need any of my coins? You must ensure that you have much change ready, or time will run out before you are ready and this would be very unfortunate, for it is important to say goodbye to friends in the proper way."

"No thanks," said Rob, jingling the coins in his hand. "I think I have enough."

"Hello?" said Alana.

Rob was pleased that it was she who picked up the phone "Hi, Alana."

"Well, hello, stranger. How was your day in London?"

"Great. I spent it with my new friend Anil. But I miss you."

"I miss you too. So why don't you come back to Bath?" Alana invited. "Can't you extend your ticket?"

"It's one of those cheap charters."

"Too bad!" she said.

A feeling of warmth flushed through Rob.

He told her all about sightseeing in London. "This damn phone is pinging in my ear."

"Put in another ten p., Rob."

"Damn! What does ten p. look like?"

"Oh Rob. Look on the back for a '10'."

"All I can find is this big coin shaped like a stop sign, and it doesn't fit in the hole."

"That's a fifty p. coin, silly. It won't work."

Rob spoke quickly to get his words in. "Bye – I'll write – love –"

The phone went dead.

Anil was refolding his clothes when Rob entered the room. "How was your phone call?"

"It was OK. But the phone ran out, like you warned," Rob said. "I was so flustered I couldn't get the coins to work."

"So how are you feeling?"

"Oh, I'm fine."

"Are you truly?"

Rob looked at his friend, who was staring at him intently.

"I feel pretty crappy."

"That's very good. You are human."

"Yeah, I guess I am," said Rob reflectively. "I guess I'll pack up now."

Downstairs, Mrs. Grimes was checking in some fresh travellers, but she left them to settle up with Anil and Rob.

"I never 'old up me guests," she said. "They have their aeroplanes to catch. So ye nice fellas have a safe journey home," she said. "'Twas nice havin' ye in the establishment. Quiet boys, them were," she said to her new customers, holding up Rob and Anil as examples.

"Thanks," said Rob.

"Thank you," said Anil. "This was a very nice home for us in London. If you ever visit the Calcutta Homeless Shelter, I will ensure that you are shown the same hospitality.

"Ho!" shouted Mrs. Grimes with glee. "I hope it'll not come to that for Mrs. Grimes, to be starvin' in India."

Anil and Rob laughed along with her and went outside. They put their bags down on the patch of grass that was Mrs. Grimes' front garden and sat on the steps. A breeze brought welcome relief from the heat of their room.

"It is very pleasurable here on the step, is it not?"

"Yes, Anil," said Rob. "I'm enjoying the fresh air."

"And what else are you thinking about?"

"Nothing, really. Just about how good the air feels hitting my face."

"You are not thinking about the urgent necessity to get to the airport early or some other requirement?" Anil quizzed.

"No, I guess I'm not," said Rob, realizing that he was not fretting about how he was going to get to the airport or what to do in the next hours ahead, but purely enjoying the moment.

"You are learning, my friend," Anil said.

"Maybe I am," said Rob hopefully.

As Anil and Rob sat at the cafeteria in the airport, Rob noticed the busyness that surrounded them. People were moving in all directions trying to get where they wanted to go. Some were searching frantically for tickets and others were urging their loved ones to hurry.

"What time does your flight leave, Anil?"

"Eight o'clock," said Anil.

"That's really soon!" said Rob, then calmed his concern. There would be plenty of time to say goodbye. "I want to thank you for hanging with me," he said.

"Yes, it was a pleasure to have your company, and no ropes," he said with a chuckle. "But seriously. You are an excellent disciple of life and I believe you have much to look towards."

"What do you mean?"

"For a long time you have lived in a small circle. You knew only those things that were found in the circle. But I believe that you have now walked out of the circle and want to keep walking. I envy you."

"What! You must be joking, Anil. You are so lucky to have been surrounded by people like Sri Rama Mata." Rob felt a momentary resentment towards his mother for the chaotic environment she had provided for him.

"It is true I have had many excellent teachers and role models, but for this reason life has been easy for me, and will continue to be. My inner development will continue at an even pace. But you have so much to discover that your path of discovery is a great adventure, with fireworks lighting up all around."

"Things do seem pretty explosive right now. Every day I sort out something new or put a new piece in the puzzle."

"Focus on inserting each piece of the puzzle, and the whole will appear someday," Anil said sagely.

"Hmm. That's deep."

"Perhaps I get carried away," said Anil sheepishly. "I believe it is time for me to go to the aeroplane now."

"I'll write you and tell how my great adventure is going."

"I wait eagerly to hear from you, my friend," Anil said, shaking Rob's hand. "Live from now on as if this were your second life, in which you can change all the things that made you unhappy."

"I'll try."

Anil gave Rob one last bit of wisdom. "Remember, Rob, that you cannot hide from your suffering. Face it with all of your courage. It will show you the right path. It will be your guide in life. Embrace your suffering and you will find great happiness and fulfilment."

Rob watched each step Anil took down the airport corridor. They were soft, angel-like steps. Just as he was to turn the corner he looked back and gave Rob a radiant smile and a graceful wave.

Rob clasped his hands and assumed a *Sanchin* stance, then bowed by moving his heels together and bending deeply from the waist. As he came up, Anil raised his hand once more and vanished.

Chapter 52

Dear Anil,

I was happy to get your letter. It was so exciting to see the envelope with an Indian stamp on it – felt like you were right here!

I'm glad you're finding your work for the homeless shelter inspiring. I can imagine how hot it is in Calcutta, wandering around in the streets all day long feeding the hungry, though I'm sure you are coping with it well. The weather here these days is blistering hot, though nothing like where you are, I'm sure. When it gets really hot I try to remember your advice about how you have to have hot to have cold.

Anyhow, this evening I am enjoying the cool air, since I worked the whole day under the sun at my house-painting job. Then I went to karate class, where I get awfully sweaty because there isn't much circulation in the dojo and I have been trying pretty hard this past month at the drills. I have been throwing myself into them with effort and hopefully some of the other virtues as well like concentration and patience, etc.

It looks like maybe the virtues are paying off, based on what happened tonight. I was about to leave when one of the other students called my name and said Sensei was looking for me. So I went into Sensei's office, and he said he was submitting my name to the Dan Test Board for my black belt in three weeks. When I got home I told my dad and he called my mother and she called her friends Bud and Jeannie and they're all going to take me out to dinner after-

wards whether I get it or not. But I know I will!

House-painting is pretty good too. I am working on my inner being the whole time, trying to pay attention to every stroke of the paintbrush on each square foot of siding on every house.

Anyhow, I wanted to thank you for everything you taught me in our day in London. I will remember that day forever. But hopefully I will get to see you before then,

Sincerely,

Rob

Hi Alana,

It made me really happy just talking to you on the phone last night. See, there I am, expressing another feeling! I'm also excited we made plans to be in some of the same classes in the fall, since this time I won't have to be so nervous about sitting next to you! Philosophy of Mind should be interesting, but probably hard because we will have to think a lot about abstract stuff like what we know and how we learn, etc.

I'm certainly learning a lot these days. Life is pretty good since I started trying to live in the moment like we talked about. Also, Mom is sober and still asking lots of questions about my life(!) She is so excited that I have a girlfriend that every day she wants to know what our plans are for the future! I tell her we are taking it day by day.

Anyhow, I wanted to say something that was hard to put into words when I was in Bath. Everything in my life seems to be getting better every day. I feel a special feeling that I have not felt for a long time, maybe since I was a child. For once I like being alive and I feel good about the future, and that every breath from now on is going to be a dragon's breath – I'll explain later.

Anyhow, I miss you and can't wait to see you,

Love,

Rob